JULIAN & SHAW

On Cravenwood Block

A.D. ELLIS

Author's Note

ONE

Shaw Elliot Fenton

She was beautiful.

Her smile lit up the room.

Her laughter like music.

But every year without her made it harder and harder to remember what she looked like. To remember that smile. Her laughter.

I'd watched as she drove away from the school on the last day I ever saw her.

At age ten, I was more concerned with heading inside to see my friends and read my books—always my books.

I should have given her one last hug.

She never made it to her job as a dental hygienist.

A car accident.

Dead.

My mother was dead.

And I was alone.

The dream morphed into a collage of images from my life over the fourteen years since I'd lost my mother. A lovely foster family—also ripped away from me. Pain and fear at the hands of the pastor father of the next foster family. The kind clerk at the ER who suspected my *clumsiness* wasn't the whole story after one too many times of being brought in for bumps, bruises, and breaks. The mediocre families I lived with from fifteen to eighteen.

And then—

I woke up in a warm, clammy sweat. The cheap motel's scratchy sheets clinging to me as the ancient air conditioning unit kicked on, spitting chunks of ice as it squealed and blasted cold air into the damp room.

The dim bathroom light bathed the dingy room in shadows as I ran my hands through my hair, trying to push aside the dream.

The dreams weren't new.

I'd had them ever since my mom died.

Each bad situation added to them.

Each even worse situation just piling on.

I usually dreamed of my mom and my shit luck ranging from her death to the loss of my first foster family to the abuse before I turned eighteen *or* the crappy situations I'd found myself in since becoming an official adult. My dreaming brain didn't often find it necessary to submerse me into *both* bad dreams.

The shitty motel I'd been holed up in was part of my crappy adult scenario, but I hadn't yet given up hope it would be the beginning of something better for me. At twenty-four, a bookworm and a dreamer at heart, I knew I had a shit ton of baggage—read that as trauma, but *baggage* made me feel less damaged—but I also knew things had to turn around at some point.

Right?

The situation I'd found myself in between eighteen and twenty-four was one I could have avoided, but I wasn't sure what my other options would have been. While I didn't *love* where I'd been in those years, I also didn't regret it because I'd been able to save up a very decent amount of money. True, a couple instances during that time period had been ugly, but I wanted to believe I was on the other side of all that now.

I'd left it behind, moved across the country, and I was determined to find my happiness. Not that I thought shelters, motels, kitchen work, and temp jobs were where my happiness lay, but each day was a new chance to put my past further behind me and look forward to something I'd never had.

Being happy.

Being wanted.

Being loved.

I had those things once, long ago.

And I was going to have them again.

I didn't know *how*, but I was going to have them.

I glanced at my phone.

Eight a.m.

With a yawn and a stretch—regretting the dream which had stolen an extra hour of sleep from me—I got up and went to shower.

While the shelters I'd stayed in were free, there was something soothing about a room to myself. Not having to share the bathroom with ten other people. A hot shower with no one waiting their turn.

The money I'd saved up wouldn't last forever—and I was nothing if not frugal in my spending—but the motel I'd happened upon was dirt cheap and gave me time to gather myself as I moved from my last temp job to whatever lay ahead.

In the past year, I'd worked in a hospital kitchen, taken night classes to earn data entry certification, and left behind the only life I'd ever known.

Wiping the condensation from the mirror, I took in my golden-brown eyes and dark brown hair. My skin was what people often described as olive and I tanned easily, taking after my mother's complexion—Mom never talked about my dad, I never asked, and then it was too late. The tattoos on my arms and chest had been at the urging of my first employer when I was eighteen. He'd footed the bill and I didn't hate them—maybe only didn't love some of the memories they stirred.

Not planning on any official job interviews that day, I left the day's growth on my chin and jaw. It wasn't truly *scruff*, but it was the best I could do. The goal for today was to explore the area while looking for a suitable job and place to live.

After brushing my teeth and styling my hair, I pulled on a pair of jeans, black t-shirt, and black Vans. Checking to be sure I had my wallet and phone along with my laptop and charger in the backpack I carried, I pocketed the hotel key and pulled the door closed behind me.

It was just nine in the morning, but the city of Midtown was already awake. The day before, I'd spent time in the large eastside Midtown library and read up on the area. I didn't have a library card yet, but I was able to browse the shelves, read in a little nook for a while, and look up articles. One public-interest piece had gone on and on about how great one area of the city was, Cravenwood Block.

From what I'd read, about twenty-five years earlier, a man named Robert Cravenwood got pissed about a proposed demolition of buildings which would make way for a parking garage. Mr. Cravenwood—as a gay man, I had to chuckle at the name—anyway, he bought the buildings and the land. He restored a few buildings, rebuilt a few, and brought the area back to life. The article suggested he'd named it after himself, but conceded it was possible people just started using his name for the area, but Cravenwood was born. It wasn't a town, but the city of Midtown named the street running down the middle of the block Cravenwood Avenue. From my understanding, many of the businesses now used Cravenwood or *cravin'* in their name.

The author of the article explained the area referred to as Cravenwood Block was like a little bubble inside a bubble. Midtown wasn't a super large city, it bordered between a large town and small city, but they claimed living and working in Cravenwood seemed to make everything feel smaller, safer, and more connected.

Smaller, safer, and more connected sounded perfect to me after a lifetime of loss and feeling unwanted.

Another article discussed the popularity of living and working on Cravenwood Block—suggesting both jobs and apartments were difficult to come by—but the article had been written a few years ago and hinted toward a prediction that both jobs and apartments would slowly become more available as certain chunks of the area's population got older, got married, had kids, and moved to the suburbs.

Maybe my timing was just right.

As I approached the area referred to as Cravenwood Block, I noticed a library. It wasn't as big as the Midtown library I'd visited the day before, but the Midtown West Branch was quaint—I immediately pictured myself securing a library card as soon as I had a place to live and spending hours in the old block building. Or at least getting hooked up with their e-reader system so I could read on my phone. While a paperback was almost always my format of choice, I definitely appreciated the convenience of having books on my phone.

Making a note to stop in and look into getting a card, I crossed the street and found myself almost immediately transported. The whole area had a different feel to it and I wanted to stay there forever.

Trying to rein myself in—I didn't need to get my hopes up and find them crushed when things didn't work out, I had a brief respite from needing to work, but I couldn't be jobless and homeless indefinitely—I decided a walk around the two-block area was my first order of business.

The first business I noticed was a little coffee shop named Cravin'-a-Cup and I decided then and there I'd walk the blocks and return for breakfast and kill a bit of time. Next door was Cravings—a bakery—but it appeared to be under construction.

As my block browsing continued, I took in a flower shop, grocery, a tattoo shop—Cravenwood Ink Designs—and I briefly wondered if I'd ever be in the market for more tattoos. There was a diner, a health center, a gym, Cravin' Cuts—a hair stylist.

The bar—Cravenwood Tap—would maybe be a good place for lunch if I stuck around for the whole day. Or the diner. My tour around the area finished by taking in a pet shop, a playground, and an education center.

The two biggest buildings on the blocks faced each other and took up one entire side of each block. Cravenwood Apartments—from what I could tell, they were called Cravenwood Apartments Tower A and Tower B, which was slightly weird since they were only three stories tall and definitely not towers—were gorgeous and I immediately wanted to beg someone to let me live there.

Rolling my eyes at my thoughts, I made my way back to the coffee shop.

How much would I love to get a nice warm drink on winter mornings? An icy treat on hot summer afternoons? All while happily working at a job I enjoyed.

Dreams, man.

I had real dreams.

"Good morning," a pretty blond man called from the behind the counter as I opened the door.

The scent of coffee and sweet cinnamon immediately

curled around me and I had the strangest feeling of *home*. The sensation rattled me for a moment—I hadn't felt truly *home* since my mom died.

"What can I getcha?" the man—his name tag said Leighton—asked with a smile.

"Can the Cravin'-a-Cup travel mug get discounted refills on hot chocolate?" I asked. Yes, I was maybe setting myself up for a crash-and-burn by presumptuously buying a travel mug when I very likely wouldn't be staying on this lovely little block, but what the hell. I'd either save money on future hot chocolates or I'd have a nice cup to remember the brief moment of hope.

"Sure does. Not a coffee drinker?" Leighton asked.

"No. Love the smell, just not the taste. Mom and I used to drink hot chocolate so it stuck." I mentally calculated the cost of a drink, a sandwich, and a pastry. "Cinnamon roll or scone?"

"The cinnamon rolls are to die for, but if you're going with something sweet like hot chocolate, the scone would be a nice balance. The lady opening the bakery next door has worked here for a few years—she's amazing. I've never tasted anything she made that wasn't delicious."

"Ouch, is that going to hurt business?" I asked.

He laughed. "No, no. She's going to be our supplier. Having her own place just means she can provide more items and take special orders. She decided to do it after years of people here asking for bulk orders of her treats. She won't be taking our customers—she's not allowed to sell coffee," he said with a grin. "But the shops will be connected with a little walk-thru door, I think it will be a great set-up."

I placed my order, grateful the meal didn't go over the daily budget I'd allowed myself. "Is it cool to charge up my laptop and do some work for a while?" I asked, assuming the shop got a lot of people hanging out and doing work, but figured it was better to ask before being seen as a nuisance.

"Sure thing. Find yourself a seat and I'll get your order right out to you." He gave a friendly wink before moving on to the next customer.

I settled in at a spot in the corner with an outlet, plugged my charger in, and opened my laptop. A few minutes later, Leighton brought my sandwich, scone, and hot chocolate.

"I'll be around to check on you, wave me down if you need anything," he said.

For a moment, I just took in the lovely little shop.

The day wasn't cold, but I could picture how warm and cozy the place would be on a winter day. After my mom died, I lost my foster family, and I was bounced from place to place, I technically became homeless. But I'd never suffered through nights on the street, battling the elements, or hunger.

And for that, I was grateful.

While a lot of my years after my mom died weren't the best, I knew I'd been lucky. I scoffed as I unwrapped my breakfast sandwich. Okay, *lucky* wasn't the right word. I'd suffered two tremendous losses, been abused, and thought of as disposable—an afterthought. But I could have been hungry, cold, and trying to live without necessities.

So, yeah, I'd had it better than some.

My decision at eighteen, while leaving me with a few extra carry-ons along with my baggage, had allowed me to feed myself and stay off the streets. I'd worked my ass off—I chuckled humorlessly at the unintended pun—to earn and save money so I could one day strike out on my own with a job I enjoyed and a place to live. If my past couch surfing while gritting my teeth and baring the decisions I'd made led to me being a functional adult, it had been worth it.

If being a functional adult came with happiness and being loved and accepted by true friends, all the better.

Sipping the hot chocolate, I smiled as I remembered all the movie nights Mom and I had. Hot chocolate, popcorn, cuddled under a blanket.

No kid should lose their mom.

Losing her at age ten meant I'd had a decade of loving her. A decade of being safe and protected and loved. But I'd been so young to be left on my own—a decade had been a blink of an eye in the grand scheme of things.

"Everything okay?" Leighton asked as he cleaned a table next to me.

I nodded. "Delicious, thanks."

"Whatcha working on?" He nodded toward my laptop.

"Brushing up my resume."

"Ohhh, nice. What type of job are you looking for?" He cocked his head and chewed on his lip. "It's not for everyone and I'd only suggest it if you truly *love* it, but I can talk to the owner about getting you on here. If you want."

I smiled. "Thanks. I like this place, but I don't think I have the right energy for this type of work. I have a certification in data entry, but my work history includes reception—front desk and department type stuff—at a hospital. I've also worked in a kitchen, but that's not what I'm wanting to do." I bit back a huff when I thought of my *other* work experience. It was difficult to balance between being grateful for the work which had saved me from being out on the streets and regretting some of the people that former job had mixed me up with.

Leighton studied me. "Yeah, I can see it. I bet you're patient and good at keeping people calm. If I had to answer phones, greet people, *and* do computer or filing work, I'd be a raging bitch."

I shrugged. "I like it." It wasn't the time or place to get into what had drawn me to working a hospital desk.

"Well, be sure to check out our community board—there are usually some job openings posted. And go to the apartments, they've got a community board where businesses post jobs." Leighton, who seemed to always be smiling, gave me a wave and headed back to the counter to wait on a new customer.

I spent a couple hours beefing up my resume, checking out some online job opportunities, and sipping an iced hot chocolate Leighton had talked me into trying. The community board at Cravin'-a-Cup didn't provide a lot of job leads, but I still had the board at the apartments to look at, plus, I'd emailed a few links to myself.

Around noon, I decided to take another walk around Cravenwood. I enjoyed the easy, comfortable bustle and friendliness of the people. At some point, I'd need to look into printing my resume, but I had hopes the jobs I'd be applying to would accept electronic copies.

I found a shady spot in the park and pulled out the latest fantasy story I'd been reading. After about forty-five minutes of reading, I realized I wasn't super into the story due to excitement about checking out the apartments and the job boards.

Heading to the Cravenwood apartment complex, I ignored my growling stomach and decided I'd swing by the Tap for lunch after I looked for job notices at the apartments.

As I walked into the apartment foyer area, I knew immediately I needed to force myself to stay calm and not get too hopeful. I was in love within moments of seeing just the main floor, but I had to keep reminding myself the apartments were likely set at a premium price. There was also probably a waiting list a mile long.

Feeling bolstered by the friendly smiles of the people

coming and going, I wandered to the community bulletin board area and perused the flyers regarding job openings.

Pet shop.

Diner.

Gym.

Barber.

Grocery.

All places which were hiring, but nothing really caught my attention.

I'd made a promise to myself—way back when the bastard pastor I had as a foster dad beat me over and over—I'd get a job in a healthcare setting or somewhere similar, maybe like a school, where I could be first-line in recognizing abuse and helping to put a stop to it.

The lady at the hospital front desk had saved my life that day. Maybe the pastor wouldn't have ever killed me, but his constant abuse would have eventually taken everything from me.

When that desk worker finally put two and two together with the number of times she'd seen me and made a report, the rest of my life had begun.

True, things had gone from bad to not great and back to bad a few times, but she got me away from that asshole and I'd never forgotten it.

I was kind, patient, caring, and good at organization, being polite in person and on the phone, and had good computer skills. I wanted a job where I could put all of it into practice and maybe help people who were suffering the way I had been back then.

As I continued to peruse, I saw the corner of a flyer covered by a poster for a bus trip to an apple orchard.

My heart fluttered as I read it.

Cravenwood Health Center.

Front desk/Reception.

Greet patients, answer phone calls, manage the waiting room.

Computer skills required for light data entry.

Signing bonus.

I yanked the sign from the board and fought the urge to hug it to my chest.

Knowing I *should* scan the QR code and replace the sign, I stuffed it in my pocket. I didn't know how long the flyer had been up there, but I didn't want anyone else getting to that job before me.

It was a dream come true.

Even if it wasn't a forever career, it was exactly what I'd been looking for and would be the perfect position to build my resume.

My head buzzed with ideas, possibilities, and next steps.

When I caught sight of the wall of mailboxes, my mind immediately jumped to the fact I desperately needed to get a PO Box.

Maybe you could get the job and a place here and not even need a PO Box.

The thought was bouncing in my head before I even had time to guard against it. It made sense, but it also required *a lot* to happen before even being a possibility.

Next to the mailboxes, a large aerial photo of Cravenwood Block hung on the wall. Beside it two large printouts, the whole display artfully grouped. One printout showed a floorplan of a sample apartment. The other was a collage of photographs from inside an apartment. A framed piece of paper announced tours of the apartments were available and listed a contact email and phone number.

Oh.

My.

God.

I wanted to go tour an apartment right that very moment.

But I had to get myself grounded.

I was already letting my head and heart get way too far ahead of reality.

My stomach grumbled.

A sign I needed to take a step back, get something to eat —although, how I was already hungry after a great breakfast was beyond me—and give myself time to think.

I'd need to skip restaurant meals the next day or so after splurging twice in one day, but the delicious aroma teasing my senses the moment I walked into Cravenwood Tap told me I'd made the right choice.

The place wasn't super busy, but it had the look of just surviving the lunch rush. Several tables needed cleaned and employees were hastily making their way through the mess.

Glancing toward the bar, I caught the eye of the bartender, and he waved me over. "Full menu over here if you don't mind a stool rather than a chair," he said with a welcoming grin.

Seriously, was Cravenwood really such a friendly place or was my heart just determined to see only the good? I'd left behind a variety of memories—some mediocre, some painful —and this place had my gut feeling like I'd stepped into the first day of the rest of my life.

The rest of my *happy* life.

Not just scraping by.

Not just surviving.

Living, thriving, and *happy*.

I couldn't remember the last time I'd been happy.

That wasn't true.

I was happy for ten years until my mom was taken from me.

And I was determined—for her memory and for me—to be happy again.

Just so happened my heart had decided Cravenwood Block was the place to make that happiness a reality.

"Stool is fine," I answered as I slid onto the barstool.

"I'm Lucas," he said, holding out his hand to shake. The man was gorgeous. Fit, but not overly muscular. Scruff on his face, but it looked purposeful, not just like he'd not had time to shave. Dark brown eyes, fair skin with a smattering of freckles, and dark red hair—too dark to be *ginger*, too light to be *auburn*.

"Shaw," I said, returning the handshake.

"You drinking today? Or just eating?"

I knew the day's spending would bite me in the ass when I was eating crackers on a cot at whatever shelter I could find, but it felt like a celebration day.

Which was stupid because nothing had happened except the very slim possibility of a job and a place to live.

Throwing caution to the wind, I glanced at the drink menu. "Do you have any ciders on tap?"

Lucas pointed out the three ciders on tap and gave a little run-down of each.

I ordered the one he claimed was the most popular.

"What would you like to eat?" he asked as he slid a tall glass in front of me.

The menu boasted several appetizers, pizza, and a few standard sandwiches. It was obvious the place was for drinking and dancing, food wasn't their specialty, but you could get the basics.

"I'll take the fish sandwich, cheese and pickle. Tartar sauce on the side please. Slaw and fries."

"Sounds good, I'll get the order in." Lucas disappeared for a bit as voices and the clang of dirty dishes being piled into tubs and taken to the back for washing filled the air.

I checked my phone. It wasn't the newest model, but it had calls, texting, email, and internet—although, I was super stingy with my data and tried to only use Wifi when available.

"You new to the area?" Lucas asked when he returned from placing my order, picking up a towel to dry glasses.

"Yeah," I said. "I'm hoping to find a job and a place to live, I like this place."

Lucas's eyes sparkled. "It's great here." His gaze traveled to the door and his face lit up. "Hey," he said to the approaching man, walking out from behind the bar to hug him.

The new arrival was equally gorgeous and they looked magazine-ready together despite Lucas being in simple jeans and a t-shirt and the other guy being in scrubs.

"Shaw, this is my best friend, Dean. Dean, our new friend, Shaw." Lucas slapped Dean on the back and returned to his spot behind the bar as Dean took the stool next to me.

Best friend?

Interesting.

I would have placed money on them being partners.

Dean had intense blue eyes, a strong jawline, short, light brown hair, and a soft, friendly smile.

"Nice to meet you," Dean said. "Be careful, this one will talk your ear off if you let him."

I chuckled. "That's okay." Honestly, I hadn't had the chance to just chat with anyone in so long, I kinda liked the idea of someone talking my ear off. I gestured toward Dean's scrubs. "You a doctor?"

He nodded. "Yeah, I work at the health center. Been a busy morning for some reason. Lots of breaks and puking." He grimaced. "You new around here?"

"Yeah," I said as Lucas placed my food in front of me. "Hoping to get a job and a place to live." I pulled the flyer from my pocket, not wanting to assume the guy could do anything for me just because he worked at the health center, but hoping all the same. "You know anything about this job posting?"

Dean took the paper and studied it. "Definitely. We've had three people in the position in the past three months—none of them have lasted more than a couple weeks. It's not like an ER at a huge hospital, not terribly busy, but we've just not been able to find the right person. You interested?"

"Very. I don't live around here yet, but this is exactly the type of job I'm looking for," I answered, swirling a fry in ketchup.

Dean pulled out his phone and clicked on the notes app. "Tell me a bit about yourself and I'll put in a good word with the lady hiring."

"Really?" I didn't even care my voice squeaked.

"Sure. If it's the type of job you're looking for, it makes sense you'd be good at it. Name? Phone number? Qualifications? Experience?"

"Shaw Elliot Fenton," I said before I rattled off my phone number and waited for Dean to tap it into his phone. "I don't actually have an address just yet," I said with a wince, "but I have a certification in data entry. I've worked in a hospital kitchen, but my related work experience is working the front desk in the pediatrics department in a hospital out west— S.A. Johnson Memorial Hospital. I also worked the main front desk at St. Mary's Hospital."

"You can use our address," Lucas said.

"For real?" I asked, feeling like I was in a dream.

"Sure. It's not like they're going to *need* your address until you're hired. We're moving into the apartments soon, but we already have a mailbox," Dean answered. He checked over his phone. "Sounds like you've got the right experience. Have you submitted your resume and the application?"

"Not yet, but I planned to do it later today."

"Here, let me give you my phone number. As soon as

you've submitted your application, text me so I know and I'll tell Cheryl to take a look." Dean sent me a text so I'd have his number.

"We can give you the name of the apartment manager where we're going to be living. Not sure they've got a room in the unit we'll be in, but maybe they've got something else?" Lucas suggested.

I bit my lip. "What's the rent like?"

Dean and Lucas caught each other's eye and smirked.

"It's very doable," Lucas said. "Definitely don't assume it's too much. We've worked here for a couple years, figuring the CATs were too pricey, but we recently found out they're very affordable."

"CATs?" I asked.

"Cravenwood Apartment Towers. There are two of them, an A and a B. *Towers* is the wrong word for the buildings, but it's what they're called," Dean explained as he sent me a contact for Julian Barrows, the apartment manager. "I'll let Julian know you're going to contact him, that okay?"

"Yeah, that's perfect. Beyond perfect."

Lucas, Dean, and I chatted a bit more.

Dean reminded me to text him once I'd applied and told me to contact Julian.

As if I could forget either of those things.

Floating on Cloud Nine back to the hotel—knowing I'd need to downsize to a shelter soon in order to save money for rent—trying my best not to get too hopeful, I couldn't help but think maybe, just maybe, things were looking up for me.

TWO

Julian Joseph Barrows

"HELLO?" I answered my phone while walking between CATs A and B to work on a jiggly door handle for a resident. I was the apartment manager—and luckily had an assistant manager—but I ended up taking on quite a few of the maintenance requests myself despite having a two-man maintenance crew.

"It's Dean Pierce," the man on the other end of the phone said. "Hoping I didn't overstep, but Lucas and I ran into a guy today who's trying to get a job at the health center and is looking for a place to live. Name's Shaw. Seems like a great guy, maybe down on his luck, but Lucas and I both liked him right away," Dean explained. "Anyway, I'm going to put in a good word for him at the health center for the front desk position. Hope it's not a problem, but we gave him your number in hopes of maybe helping him find a place."

"Yeah, not a problem," I said. While there was technically a waiting list for the Cravenwood Apartments, most of the folks were waiting on a specific unit or had already found a place. The third floor of each tower was reserved for those who worked on the block and had a bit more leeway with taking in residents. "We've got some spaces open. I can give him a tour and see if he's interested."

"I'm guessing money is a bit tight for him right now, so hopefully he can swing the rent," Dean explained.

"Tell him how cute he is." I heard Lucas holler in the background.

Dean laughed. "Lucas would like you to know Shaw is super cute."

I chuckled as I took the stairs to the second floor to find the jiggly door handle. "Good to know. Is Lucas staking a claim?" From what I'd learned of the two best friends, Lucas was bisexual and Dean was straight—although, seeing them together made me wonder about whether one or both of them were completely oblivious to how much they didn't seem like *just friends*.

Clearly, I was on speaker because Lucas's voice came through again. "No, but I feel like there's a certain apartment manager who may be interested."

I scoffed. I hadn't known the two men long, but they were easy to like and I knew they'd fit into the crew we already had living in the apartment. "I don't make it a habit of coming on to the residents." In reality, I'd come into my sexuality later than many and I'd realized soon after I wasn't the type to sleep around. Not only did I want something more permanent, I needed to feel a connection to the man I took to bed along with being attracted to more than just his body.

I'd had sexual partners and I'd dated, but I hadn't found fulfillment in the past and often worried I never would. Maybe the guy I was looking for—and I didn't even know what type of guy that would be—just didn't exist.

Outside of sex, I pretty much got everything I needed from great family and friends. I'm not saying I didn't want sex, but I wasn't longing for it. And honestly, sex with someone I didn't know or didn't feel a connection to just wasn't something I was looking for.

My dad, Roger, lived nearby and we saw each other often.

My brother—he was technically a half-brother, but I didn't see it that way—had come to live with us when I was in my late teens and he was just a child. Ollie was a strange mix of little brother I wanted to protect and best friend I enjoyed spending time with.

So far, the apartment we shared had Ollie and me, Leighton—our barista friend—and a new guy named Jett who Leighton was infatuated with.

Lucas and Dean were in the process of moving in.

Ollie was panting after Sebastian—a guy at work—and thrilled to have him moving in.

Technically, I could have moved Sebastian into the room connected to mine, but I had a feeling Ollie would have strangled me, so I'd told Sebastian the only room available was the one connected to Ollie's.

That left the room connected to mine as the only one available in our unit.

Didn't mean this Shaw guy had to live with us. I could offer him a couple other spots on the third floor. Somewhat selfishly, I wanted to keep that empty room, but I knew filling it was better for business.

I'd wait to see what kind of vibe I got from Shaw if and when he contacted me.

Three hours later, my phone rang as I was finishing up some paperwork in my office in Tower A. For the most part, the residents followed rules and got along surprisingly well—I had a feeling it was because the apartments were so sought after and housed so many Cravenwood Block employees who took pride in our little bubble of Midtown—but I occasionally had complaints and violations to deal with. I counted myself lucky our bank dealt with all of the financials as far as rent and late payments.

"Hello?" I said, leaning back in my chair and rubbing my neck after nearly an hour of staring at the computer screen.

"Hi, um…" The voice on the other end of the line was soft but determined and I sat up a little straighter, immediately and inexplicably drawn in. "My name is Shaw Fenton. I got your number from Dean and Lucas. They said you might have an apartment available?"

"Yeah, Dean let me know you might be calling. Would you want a tour? What's the job situation looking like? Some of the apartments are only available for Cravenwood Block employees, but if you're working here you get a discount on rent." True, it wasn't a huge discount, but it was still a perk to living and working on the block.

I swore I could hear the smile in Shaw's voice when he said, "Oh, um, as long as my background check comes through—which I have no reason to think it won't—I'll be starting at the health center at the end of the week. When Dean says he'll put in a good word, he means it. I applied and they called right away, interviewed me, and asked me to start. I'm slightly concerned about why the position was open and why they were so insistent I start so quickly, but Dean says it's just because the last three people haven't been a good fit. He says the job isn't bad if that's the type of work I want to do. And it is." He paused and I imagined him biting his lip. I wanted to see him and know if his cheeks tinted pink when he was embarrassed. "Oh my god, I'm so sorry. That was way more information than you needed to know."

I chuckled. "All good. I'm glad you got the job. What time works for you for a tour?"

"Tomorrow morning?"

"How about ten? Most of the residents in the unit should

be awake and gone by then, or they'll be asleep and we won't bother them."

"I can do ten."

I scribbled myself a note to add to the calendar. "Come to Cravenwood Apartment Tower A. I'll meet you by the elevator. If I'm not there, feel free to text to let me know when you arrive. I'll probably have on jeans, work boots, and a denim shirt." I wasn't known for my high fashion, but Leighton swore I did good things for a pair of jeans and was maybe the only man he knew who could make a denim shirt look *fabulous*—his words, not mine.

"Perfect. See you then."

We said a polite goodbye and I ended the call.

And proceeded to be completely useless the rest of the day.

I wanted to track down Dean and Lucas and ask them what Shaw looked like, but I knew if I did the guys would be onto me in a split second. We maybe didn't know each other *well*, but it would be a dead giveaway.

And I wasn't ready to let them in on what was going on in my head.

Mostly because I didn't even understand what was going on.

It was ridiculous, but Shaw's voice had done something to me.

I wanted to know what he looked like.

Wanted to hear him talk.

Wanted to know everything about him.

And desperately wanted him to qualify for the apartment so he'd be around.

Hell, if needed, I'd break something just to have to go to the health center and see him at work.

Fuck.

What the hell was up with me?

I'd never once found myself thinking about someone after just hearing their voice.

Maybe I was just letting Lucas get to me with his comment about how cute Shaw was.

Or maybe it was Dean's words about how Shaw was maybe a bit down on his luck.

Either way, I was being ridiculous.

I'd meet up with the guy in the morning and show him the apartment.

Nothing more.

———

AFTER A NIGHT of tossing and turning, I finally gave up and stumbled from bed.

"Hey, baby doll," Leighton said as I walked into the kitchen. "No offense, boo, but you look like something the cat dragged in."

"Didn't sleep well," I answered.

"Eeeww, sorry." Leighton took a swig of juice. "You wanna walk me to work and I'll get you a nice coffee to start your day?"

Needing caffeine, I nodded. "Sure, let me get dressed." None of the guys in the apartment were super modest, but some wore more revealing sleepwear than others. Ollie, Jett, and I were usually in boxers or boxer briefs, often times throwing on a tank or t-shirt if we were going to be around the group for more than just a trip to the kitchen. Sebastian hadn't been with us long, but he seemed to be leaning toward the same.

Leighton was definitely more of an exhibitionist, especially since Jett had moved in. Leighton had taken to wearing skimpy bottoms any time he thought Jett might be around.

Those two were definitely dancing around something—and I wanted the best for Leighton, but I had to admit I was worried he'd crash and burn. Again.

As I made my way to my room, I heard Leighton greet Jett.

"Good morning, honey bunches," Leighton cooed.

"No," Jett groused. The man *looked* dark and dangerous—dark hair, dark eyes, dark scruff, and covered in tattoos—but I'd realized he wasn't a bad guy, just didn't really seem to know how to fit in with people. And he was definitely in the *finding himself* stage of his life, but I don't think anyone could miss the way his eyes lingered on Leighton even when he was trying to be tough and detached.

"Get dressed and walk with Julian and me to the Cup. I'll make your favorite black coffee and you can wake yourself up as you walk back home," Leighton told Jett as I came back into the kitchen.

Jett looked as if he wanted to protest, but he also looked at Leighton as if blinded by the bright goodness of the kid—like he had no clue what was happening, but he couldn't look away—and just grumbled something close to an agreement.

Sebastian and Ollie emerged from their shared rooms, both dressed for work and looking ready for the day. My little brother had been in for the shock of his life recently when he met Sebastian and realized his new boss was the guy he... well, let's just say it was awkward.

Luckily, Bash—the name he liked to be called by his friends and we'd all easily adopted—hadn't held the situation against Ollie, probably because he was desperate for a place to live.

I got the feeling the two of them would be great for each other, and that wasn't *just* because Ollie panted after Bash like a dog begging for a bone. Bash liked to pretend he didn't notice Ollie, but I'd seen a few of the looks the older man gave my little brother. There was definitely something there. Now, whether they—or more to the point, *Bash*—let anything happen was a whole other story.

"You two want to walk with us to get coffee? I'm heading to work. Julian didn't sleep well, Jett needs a jolt to that gorgeous ass to get his day started, and you two—well, you two don't *look* like you need caffeine. You actually look good enough to eat or walk the runway, but you can still get coffee." Leighton pulled Ollie into a hug. "Butterfly pea flower tea for my bestie, of course."

That's how I ended up walking down the street way too early in the morning with my four roommates. Leighton treated us all to beverages and Bash bought everyone a pastry.

Ollie and Bash headed off to the education center.

Leighton dove right into his barista work—it seriously took a special type to be that cheery in the morning and Leighton was the perfect little ray of sunshine.

"How's the shop?" I asked as Jett and I headed back to the apartment.

"Going well. I've gotten some appointments based on word of mouth, but also quite a few who've seen the open sign or found me through online ads." He sipped his coffee.

"That's great. You got an early appointment today?" It seemed kinda weird he was up so early since he often worked later in the evenings.

Something passed over Jett's face I couldn't quite read. "Nah, Leighton was loud as fuck getting ready so I woke up. Gonna go back to bed for a while."

Interesting.

And cute.

I kinda loved that Jett got up to see Leighton off to work even though he was tired. I wasn't one to ship people—sorry, that was a word Ollie and Leighton had me using—but I wasn't against seeing something spark between Jett and Leighton.

As long as Leighton wasn't hurt.

We said goodbye on the ground floor and Jett headed up the stairs. He was fit and I had no doubt taking three flights of stairs instead of the elevator was part of the reason why.

I spent the next three hours going over plans with my assistant manager, Chloe, divvying up the maintenance jobs between my crew and myself, and doing my best not to obsess over Shaw coming for a tour.

He maybe wouldn't even show up.

Appointments flaked out all the time.

But at nine-thirty, I made a quick trip up to our unit. After brushing my teeth to rid myself of coffee breath, running a hand through my soft brown hair—wondering if I should have shaved the two-day scruff—and making sure the apartment looked nice, I did a quick check of the spare room before heading back downstairs.

At nine-fifty-five, I glanced toward the door as I straightened the community announcement board, and my world shifted on its axis.

Dark hair, olive skin, dark eyes, a tiny bit of scruff, hints of tattoos.

He glanced uncertainly around the lobby area, hefting his backpack on his back and shifting a duffle on his shoulder.

An angel.

That was what he immediately made me think of.

An innocent, beautiful, fragile angel descended to Earth to walk amongst mere mortals.

But despite all that, he was also tough.

Resilient.

No matter the air of being worn down, beat up, hoping against hope, he was determined to do better, be more, *win*.

And I was gone.

I knew from the moment I laid eyes on him, I'd never be the same.

Not that I thought anything would come from it—he was at least ten years younger than me and looking for an apartment, not an older man to hit on him—but that didn't stop the pounding of my heart. It beat in a rhythm I wasn't accustomed to—having never been gut-punched just seeing a man from across the room—and I had to take a deep breath in hopes of composing myself.

His eyes traveled the room until they landed on me and my breathing hitched when he smiled.

Could a smile kill someone? Because there was a damn good chance my heart stopped the moment he smiled.

Pushing it all aside the best I could—because one, I had no desire to make a fool of myself, and two, I had no idea what to do with the insane, overwhelming feelings—I smiled back and made my way toward him.

"Shaw?" I asked.

"Hi. Julian?"

We shook hands and I ignored the heat coursing through me at the touch of his small, delicate hand in mine. He wasn't a petite person, probably about five foot eight to my even six foot, but there was just a delicate air about him. He was slim, but not skinny. There was just a softness to him, but his eyes flashed with grit and determination and I got the feeling watching him come into his own was going to be a privilege.

And there I went getting *way* too far ahead of myself.

"Nice to meet you. Ready to see the place?" I asked.

Shaw took a deep breath and pressed his lips together. "Actually, is there any way we could discuss rent and all that first? If I can't swing it, I don't want to know what I'm missing out on."

My heart ached for the kid and I crossed everything worth

crossing that the rent was within his price range. "Sure thing. Let's go to my office and see what we can figure out."

I led him to my office and opened the door. The space wasn't large, but I didn't use it often if I could keep from it. Gesturing for him to put his bags down and have a seat, I sat behind my desk and tapped my laptop to wake it up.

"Okay, let's get some information in here and see what we're looking at." I pulled up the program we used and typed in his name. "Just so you know, all the information you provide here today is completely confidential outside of the bank and the two of us."

Shaw's cheeks pinked and he bit his lip exactly the way I'd pictured the other night on the phone. Why did I want to gather this kid in my arms and hold him tight?

"Thanks," he answered softly. "I have money in the bank and good credit, I just need to make sure the rent won't be more than I can keep up with. My biggest concern is I don't have a solid history of residency and I don't have a permanent address to give you. Dean said I could use his, but it might raise a red flag if my address is the same as the place I'm wanting to move into."

"Let's see what we can do. The credit is going to weigh more than anything and I can maybe finagle some things. If you've got good credit and money to pay the rent, you should be good."

After entering a few more details, I pressed the button and turned the screen to show Shaw the monthly rent. "Now, there's a deposit and we require first and last month's rent, but the last month's rent can be split between your first four month's payments if that helps."

Shaw turned wide eyes my way. "You're joking, right?"

My stomach sank. It was too much. "Unfortunately, no. With the employee discount, that's the lowest I can go."

An almost hysterical giggle escaped Shaw's lips and he

pressed a hand to his mouth. "No, I mean you've got to be joking about the price of this place. There's no way it's that cheap. The few apartments I've looked at are half the size and twice the money."

Relief washed over me and I shrugged. "What can I say? The owner is making money, but has always indicated he wanted the places to be obtainable. It helps that eight people usually split a unit. You feel good about this amount? Want to see the space?"

Shaw grinned. "Definitely." He moved to heft his bags from the floor.

"You can leave those here, I'll lock it if you'd like."

He bit his lip, glancing at his bags. "Do you mind? Pretty much my life is in those bags, but I'd rather not lug them on the tour."

"Not a problem," I said, clicking the lock on the door and pulling it closed behind us. "Will you have a lot to move in?"

Shaw snorted. "Basically, those two bags and me is all I've got."

The kid was killing me.

Without giving it a second thought, I decided not to show him the empty room—not until I got it furnished with at least a bed.

I cleared my throat. "The unit I'm going to show you has one room completely empty so you can get an idea of how the place is set up. The single room that would be yours is being," I swallowed against the tiny lie, "um, worked on right now."

Shaw's face fell. "When would I be able to move in?"

Shit.

He likely needed the place sooner rather than later.

"Oh, it should be ready by tomorrow, no worries. Just don't want to interrupt while it's being worked on today." I pointed toward our door. "So, each of the three units on the third floor are for Cravenwood Block employees only and come with private access to the roof top—it's the same in the other tower, too." I caught the look on Shaw's face and chuckled. "Yeah, *tower* is a misnomer, but CAT A and CAT B worked, so we kept it." I unlocked the door and ushered him inside.

"What's on the rooftop?" Shaw asked, his eyes wide as he took in the living space.

"Private pool, dining area, sauna and jacuzzi, gym, and lounge area," I explained.

"This is so nice," Shaw said, brushing a hand over our large sectional couch.

"So, let me give you the rundown. Each unit has a living room, a kitchen, a laundry, four double-occupancy bedrooms sharing two bathrooms, and an additional half bathroom near the laundry room," I said, pointing toward the laundry room and small bathroom. "The bedrooms are the unique part. The original designer must have thought a lot of adults living on their own wouldn't want to share a room like kids in a dorm, so the bedrooms have one door that opens to a shared little foyer or lounge-ish area, and then each sleeping area has its own door. The sleeping area has room for a queen-sized bed, dresser, and desk. There's a built-in closet and each room shares a bathroom with the neighboring room through the lounge area." I pointed toward the colored doors around the living space. "My little brother, Ollie, Leighton, and me have all been here for a while. Jett, Bash, Lucas, Dean, and you are all coming in around the same time. I'm going to show you the green door as a model. Ollie lives with Sebastian behind the blue door. The green and blue living areas share a bathroom. You'll be in the orange door and it shares a bathroom with Leighton and Jett behind the purple door." I cleared my throat. "Full disclosure, I'm behind the orange door, so we'd be roommates."

When Shaw's eyes went wide, I wasn't sure if I was looking at dismay, curiosity, or just surprise. "But your bedroom is completely private, let me show you." I unlocked the green door and pushed it open into the little lounge type area that belonged to Lucas and Dean. "I think you met Lucas and Dean, right?"

Shaw nodded.

"This is where they're slowly moving in." I pushed open one of the bedroom doors. "So, like I said, plenty of room for a full or queen—depending on what you like to sleep on." Yes, I was totally fishing as I planned just how I was going to get a mattress purchased and delivered and set up in Shaw's room before tomorrow.

"Any bed is a good bed. Is this one a queen?" he asked and I was forever grateful Lucas and Dean had already moved most of their big items in. Shaw never had to know the room didn't actually come furnished.

"Yeah, it's a queen."

"It's a good size, but I won't complain about any bed." He moved to the built-in closet. "This is nice. I don't have enough clothes to fill it just yet, but it's nice to have the room. I need to get some extra scrubs, but the health center gave me two sets to start with." He glanced at the desk and dresser. "Do all the rooms have the same furniture or is it different?"

I sniffed and ran my hand over the back of my neck. "Um, pretty much all different. Sometimes folks don't want what's provided, so we put it in storage and they move their own belongings in." I wasn't full-on lying, some people left their furniture when they moved out and we just put it in a storage area in the basement. I knew I'd be able to find what I needed and just get a mattress bought.

All before tomorrow.

"I'm grateful for whatever is in my room." He turned

huge, deep brown eyes my way. "Wow, *my* room. That's so cool."

I knew without a shadow of a doubt the kid had a history —painful, if I had to guess—but I was glad to be even just the smallest part of his present and future as he moved away from the hurt.

Smiling, I showed him the rest of the apartment, grateful Jett was asleep and no one else was home so I didn't have to worry about them spilling the details about the rooms *not* being furnished when I very much planned on having Shaw's room at least modestly outfitted by the time he arrived tomorrow.

I walked him down the stairs. As he grabbed his bags from my office, I fought the urge to just tell him my plan and offer to let him use the couch for the night.

Where would he sleep over night? Midtown and a few surrounding areas had shelters. Or maybe he'd get a hotel. But he'd indicated he was trying to save money.

"Can I come back in the morning? I'd love to get moved in and settled before starting work," Shaw said, adjusting his backpack and hefting the duffel onto his shoulder.

"Yeah, as early as eight works for me." It dawned on me I hadn't shown him the rooftop. "Damn, I forgot the roof. I'll show you tomorrow, yeah?"

Shaw smiled and I swore I heard angels singing. "Yeah, that works great." He stuck out his hand. "Thanks. I really appreciate it."

"No problem. See you tomorrow."

I couldn't wipe the grin from my face as I returned to work.

Around noon, I took a break and popped into Cravenwood Tap for lunch. Yeah, I was hoping to catch Dean —Lucas would do in a pinch—but I also enjoyed their food.

As if I'd planned it, Dean sat at the bar eating while Lucas manned the lunch rush. Taking the stool next to Dean, I greeted them both and ordered my usual turkey wrap and applesauce—if I was eating out most days, I had to at least *try* to keep my meals moderately healthy. A burger and fries every day, at my age, wasn't going to cut it.

"You eat like you're seventy-five instead of thirty-five," Lucas teased.

"Better to be in the habit now than have to make big changes when my metabolism shits out," I said. "It's not like I eat healthy *all* the time, just don't need a big greasy burger for every lunch."

"He's got a point," Dean said. "We're closing in on thirty, wouldn't hurt to make a few healthier changes."

"We'll swim and work out more now that we've got private pool and gym access," Lucas said with a wink as he went to take an order at the end of the bar.

Images of Shaw flashed through my head. Would he enjoy the pool? Maybe he was more a sauna guy?

"What's got you all smiley?" Dean asked. The guy was a doctor and could be a bit standoffish—bordering on aloof at times—until you got to know him better. Lucas was a good buffer. I wondered for about the millionth time if the two men had ever explored anything between them, but Dean was supposedly straight, so I assumed I needed to let it go.

For real, though, maybe it was just the bond of history and friendship between them, but Lucas and Dean were electric when they were together.

"Could I ask a favor?" I sipped my water, figuring Dean was the most likely to keep things quiet and the least likely to give me shit. Sebastian would have been a close second.

"Sure, what's up?" Dean wiped his mouth and placed his napkin over his plate.

"Remember how you were saying you thought Shaw was pretty down on his luck?"

"You met him?" Dean beamed. "He's great, right? Something about him just made me want to help—and he wasn't even asking for help."

"Yeah, seems like a great guy." I grimaced. "I may have led him to believe the rooms come with furniture—he told me everything he owns is in those two bags he was carrying—so I didn't let him see his room, told him it was being worked on, and I want to get furniture carried up from the basement. Get a mattress. All before eight in the morning."

Dean stared at me for a beat and then laughed. "Lucas was so damned right. How the hell does he do that shit?"

"Do what shit?" I asked.

"He said the two of you would hit it off and went on and on about how good you'd look together."

"Nah, it's nothing like that," I protested. "Just want to give him a little boost and help him get settled before he starts the job. That was really nice of you to get him an interview."

"He landed the job himself. The hiring person said he was quite impressive." Dean finished his water. "So, you want help carrying stuff up?"

"We can use the freight elevator. What time are you off?"

"I took a half day to move the rest of our stuff in, so I'm all yours. How about you go get the mattress while I work on getting our stuff upstairs. Then we can get the furniture you want from the basement and move the mattress up." Dean smirked. "You know, if people see us, they're going to wonder what's going on. Maybe ought to let Ollie and Leighton know not to spill the beans."

"You're not wrong," I said.

"Don't tell him that. He'll get a big head," Lucas said, placing my to-go bag in front of me and snapping a towel at his best friend. "Leave me a nice tip, asshole," he told Dean, handing him his bill.

"I'm moving most of your shit in, that's tip enough," Dean teased, but he gave me a look. "Might not hurt to let him in on it so he can keep his big mouth shut."

I pinched the bridge of my nose, but filled Lucas in.

He didn't stop grinning the entire time I told him what was going on.

"I knew it," Lucas said, seeming much more interested in matchmaking than letting Shaw in on what I was doing.

I worked on paperwork for a bit while eating my lunch, then I let Chloe and the maintenance crew know I was off to run some errands.

Loading into the apartment truck—which was technically mine because it came as a perk of the job—I headed to the other side of Midtown for a mattress.

During the hour it took me to drive there, find the best quality mattress at the lowest price, help the guy load it into the truck, and drive back to Cravenwood, I proudly didn't let my imagination wander to Shaw sleeping—or doing *whatever* —on that mattress.

Okay, maybe it wandered a bit.

But I kept it mostly under control and mainly G-rated.

Or PG-13.

Fuck, okay, I maybe let it move into R and NC-17, but only for a moment.

Slamming the truck into Park, I texted Dean and asked if he was ready to meet me at the freight elevator.

Two hours later—truly, I didn't blame Dean for asking me for help with getting some of their stuff moved up as well— all of the furniture was in Shaw's room. I just needed to put the bed together and get everything arranged.

"Ollie," Leighton said from the doorway to Shaw's room, "what is your gorgeous, caring, protective big brother doing?"

"Gee, Leigh," Ollie responded and I could hear the grin in

his words, "I don't know. It would appear he's furnishing a room that comes unfurnished for a new roommate."

"Ollie," Leighton continued, his words light and teasing, "why would our dear Julian furnish a room for his new roommate?"

I pretended not to notice their play acting as I opened up my toolbox to begin working on the bed.

"Well, bestie, from what a little birdy told me, Julian's new roommate is super cute and sweet." From the corner of my eye, I saw Ollie put an arm around Leighton's shoulders. "I'm thinking Julian may have a *thang* for this new guy."

"Stop being pests," Bash told the two as he made his way into the room. "Leave the man alone to do his work."

"Yes, Daddy Bash," Leighton said with a smirk.

I straightened up from screwing together two parts of the frame. "You," I pointed to my little brother, "should be thanking me for making certain empty rooms work in your favor."

Ollie glanced at Bash and bit his lip. "Heard." His cheeks pinked. "Come on," he pulled Leighton from the room. "Let's go bug Jett."

"Those two are menaces when they're bored," Bash said with a chuckle. "You need any help?"

"Wouldn't turn it down," I said. "Need to get this room arranged tonight."

"Not to get into your business," Bash hedged, "but what's up with furnishing the room?"

I sighed, hefting the final piece of the frame into position and letting Bash drill the last screw into place. "The new guy, Shaw, was recommended by Dean and Lucas. He's the new front desk clerk at the health center. He didn't come straight out and say it, but Dean and I both got the feeling he's a bit down on his luck. I may have kinda led him to believe furniture came with the room when I realized most of what he owns fills up two bags." Putting the bed frame down and testing each corner, I shrugged. "Not a big deal. We have excess furniture stored in the basement."

"Excess mattresses, too?" I didn't miss the hint of humor in Bash's voice.

I coughed. "Nah, just didn't want the kid sleeping on the floor or stressing his finances when he's just trying to get a fresh start."

"He got a rough past?" Bash asked.

"He never came out and said anything—he's a weird mix of soft-spoken and determined, but didn't go into great details—but I'm guessing there's definite trauma of some sort." I ran a hand through my hair. "Honestly, I'm torn between being curious and really not even wanting to know how bad it is." The thought of Shaw being hurt in the past wasn't something I wanted to think about.

"It's a nice thing you're doing," Bash said, packing the drill back into the toolbox.

I got the feeling he didn't want to dwell on pasts—a lot of us in the apartment had our own heavy pasts to deal with.

"Let's hope it doesn't come back to bite me," I said.

THREE

Shaw

WAKING up in the hotel room the next day—the very last day of being essentially homeless—was a surreal feeling.

For the past fourteen years of my life, I never knew from day to day where I'd be sleeping, eating, or going to school.

The first few years after I lost my mom were as good as could be expected. My first foster family was great and things were as comfortable as they could be for a ten-year-old who'd lost his mother.

But then my foster dad—soon-to-be adoptive dad—was in a terrible accident and my life changed dramatically.

Again.

As an adult, I understood why my foster mom couldn't keep me on as a responsibility when her husband had been made a quadriplegic. But as a child who had already lost his entire life when I lost my mom, losing my foster parents—first, finding out he'd been in a wreck like the one that took my mother and then finding out I was leaving the only home I'd known for three years—it seemed the cruelest of fates.

From age thirteen to fifteen, I often woke on the couch or floor praying it had all just been a bad dream. But then, my new foster dad—the pastor at a local church—would drag me from bed. With a Bible lesson beat into me and a breakfast oh-so-lovingly prepared by my foster mom as she turned a blind eye to the abuse—what did she care? At least it was the orphan being beaten rather than her or her real children—I'd be sent off to school.

School—mainly because of the books I could escape into—was a safe haven in a lot of ways. Eight hours away from the abuse. Eight hours to learn and be told how smart I was by teachers who were mostly nice. Eight hours to eat in peace and bury myself in fictional worlds.

Sometimes, now, I wondered if those books were some of the only reasons I made it through the pain and heartache.

The years from fifteen to eighteen—after the front desk clerk at the hospital reported my foster father—weren't terrible, but I still never knew where I'd be waking up, eating, or going to school.

I'd had the best and worst of the foster care system, and if I'd learned anything, it was to always expect the unexpected.

Keeping every belonging tucked close in a bag—and feeling lucky to have a real bag instead of a trash bag. Sleeping with your arms curled through the straps and the zippers pressed close to your body. Never getting too close to kids at school because the moment you thought you had a friend, *boom* you were whisked away somewhere else.

I knew I'd actually been a fairly lucky kid—and damn, how sad was that?

I'd had complete and total love and stability from birth to age ten.

I'd had a family who helped me heal from ten to thirteen.

Thirteen to fifteen was shit—but I could always find positives like the teachers, the books, the fact that sometimes it's better the devil you know than the devil you don't.

Fifteen to eighteen was lonely, uncertain, and piled on my

anxiety—often giving me way too much time to think about the past, but also giving me time to grieve all I'd been through and all I'd lost.

Eighteen...

I shook my head and rolled from bed.

Decisions and happenings from eighteen to twenty-three were things I'd need to think of another day.

Today was moving day.

A brief wash of longing and regret ran through me and tears stung my eyes.

"I got a place all by myself, Mom," I said to the empty hotel room. "I know the past few years haven't been the best —a lot of things I wanted to experience on my own terms were taken from me—but all of that led me here." I took a deep breath and wiped away the tear. "And here feels like a really good place to be." My whisper hung in the silence, but I believed Mom knew.

Deciding there'd be no dwelling on what had happened in the past for the day, I dressed in worn black jeans, my Vans, and a faded t-shirt.

Today was the day I took hold of my life and made better things happen.

Starting with the most amazing apartment in the most amazing little bubble of Midtown.

With the most amazing, gorgeous man I'd ever seen.

Julian Barrows.

He was...

Honestly, he stole both my breath and my words.

The moment I'd seen him had me feeling all steam-rolled like in a dang cartoon.

I'd guess he was mid-thirties. Soft brown hair and brown eyes, slight wrinkles around his eyes when he smiled, and he somehow made a denim work shirt look like sex personified.

He wasn't built like a linebacker, but he was broader than

me. Only a couple inches taller than me, and while I hadn't seen his abs, I had a feeling he was inching closer to *dad bod* territory than six-pack, but he turned me on like no man ever had.

I'd known I was gay since before my mom died—well, I'd known I was *different* since then—but my sexuality had kinda taken a backseat to trauma over the past several years.

And for a recent chunk of those years, my sexuality—and sex, in general—had become a confusing part of my survival. I wanted to regain control of that aspect of my life, make decisions simply because I wanted to, not because a paycheck depended on it.

But those things would take time.

And trust in others.

And exploration.

But until then, Julian was checking all my boxes and filling my imagination with all sorts of fun.

He also had me thinking about how desperate I'd been for a positive male in my life. Sure, I'd had a couple over the years, but Julian had waltzed in with his kind, caring, strong, helpful nature and I immediately had stars in my eyes.

I wasn't sure it was a good idea to be thinking sex thoughts *and* emotional connection thoughts about a guy I'd only spent an hour with, but I knew my head and heart were all kinds of fucked-up, so I let it go.

It wasn't as if I thought Julian would see *anything* in me aside from just a renter and roommate.

And it was likely for the best if I got myself settled in and working through some shit before getting involved with anyone.

But damn, that didn't mean I couldn't lock him up tight in my head and bring him out to play when the need arose.

I'd never really gotten into daddy kink, but Julian had the whole *Daddy* thing going in a way that definitely had me interested. Strong, protective, caring—as much as I knew I probably needed to keep my distance, that man was a siren call.

Hopefully my heart wouldn't be bashed against the rocks.

Leighton smiled and waved as I walked into Cravin'-a-Cup on my way to my new place. I held my reusable travel mug in hopes of getting some hot chocolate.

"Roomie!" he called as he rushed around the counter to yank me into a friendly hug. "Your room is all ready and looks great! Julian worked so hard on it last night." Suddenly, his cheeks pinked and he bit his lip.

"Julian was doing the work? I thought he was the manager?"

Leighton shrugged. "Yeah, he is, but he does a lot of the work. He likes doing things like that." He ushered me to a table and took my mug. "Breakfast is on me this morning. I'll bring it right out."

That man was a ray of sunshine and I couldn't help but smile as he bustled away.

Checking my phone, I saw a text from Julian telling me to come to his office when I got there and he'd help me get settled.

Part of me felt as if I was using up his valuable time and he should just hand over my key or have his assistant deal with me. But I also couldn't help feeling giddy at the thought of seeing Julian and spending even a bit of time with him again.

I hadn't even let myself obsess over the fact we'd be sharing a room. True, we'd have separate sleeping areas, but only a wall separated us. We'd share a bathroom. I'd see the man daily—likely multiple times a day.

Just as Leighton headed my way, an unwanted thought slammed into me.

What if Julian was already involved with someone?

Would I have to see him with a partner?

What if he wasn't gay or bisexual?

Would he have men or women parading through our little shared space?

Shit.

I needed to get my imagination under control before I went and made a fool of myself.

"Here ya go," Leighton said as he handed me a bag and placed two drinks on the table. "For you and Julian. Breakfast sandwiches, pastries, a coffee for Julian and hot chocolate for you."

"That's too much, let me pay." I wouldn't have splurged on *all* that food, but I couldn't just take the breakfast without offering to pay.

"Nope. It's my gift. We need to hang out soon. Maybe you, me, and Ollie can go out. You like to dance?"

"No," I chuckled. "I'm more the curl up with a good book and hot chocolate type."

Leighton's eyes sparkled. "You and Julian both."

Biting my lip, I forged ahead, hoping it wasn't a mistake to trust Leighton. "Does Julian...I mean...is he involved with anyone?"

My new friend beamed. "He's not. And he's very gay— although, he came to the conclusion a bit later than some. He doesn't date a lot, hasn't been super serious about anyone I've ever known of, and he's the best guy you'll ever meet." He put his arm around my shoulder. "You can't let him know I told you, but most of the rooms aren't furnished and new renters opt to bring their own stuff. He's super happy with the furniture he found for you—" Leighton paused with a chuckle when a look of shock filled my face. "He didn't buy it all, just the mattress because eewww, but he worked hard to get it all to match as close as possible. Look, I'm not telling you this to put you on the spot or anything, I just want you to know what a good guy he is. Truly, the real deal."

"I, um, I don't even know what to say."

"Just tell him thank you. And don't tell him I told you."

"I need to pay him back—"

"No." Leighton patted my cheek. "He'll have my balls if he finds out I told you. Please, save my balls, Shaw, please? Don't tell him. Just enjoy the mattress and know he's one of the good ones."

I thanked Leighton and left the coffee shop, texting Julian I was on my way.

My heart flip-flopped in my chest as I thought of what Julian had done for me.

Part of me knew I needed to just straight up ask him about the furniture and mattress and demand I pay for whatever he'd spent.

But I didn't want to get Leighton in trouble.

And my chest was so warm and tingly from the incredibly kind gesture, I couldn't help but just smile and feel cared for.

Turned out I was quickly learning I had thing for being wanted, cared for, and protected. Who knew?

Gee, dumbass, I don't know. Who would have ever figured out a kid with no father, a dead mother, and various other trauma would be desperate for someone to show them kindness and caring?

I snorted at the thought.

Guess it didn't really take much brain power to figure that one out.

I just hoped I didn't let myself get too over my head with Julian.

The man was so helpful and kind, but I didn't need that making me think he was into me.

No, I definitely needed to keep things under control in that aspect.

———

I'D BEEN LIVING and working on Cravenwood Block for a little over a week and I was in love.

In love with my new room.

In love with my new roommates.

In love with Cravenwood—even though it made me secretly giggle every time I thought of an entire apartment full of queer men in a place called Cravenwood. For real, I wasn't the only one who laughed at that, right?

Cravenwood?

Cravin' wood.

Get it?

But I digress.

An apartment full of queer men maybe wasn't completely accurate. In getting to know the guys, I'd learned a bit about each of them. Ollie, Bash, Leighton, Julian, and I were gay. Lucas was bisexual. Jett had moved in claiming to be straight, but I'd put money on that label getting thrown out the window.

And Dean said he was straight.

I didn't like saying *said he was straight* because if a person said they were straight, you should believe them until they indicated otherwise—which they may or may not ever do. But Dean—and Jett—whether by their words or just the lust-filled looks in their eyes when they looked at Lucas and Leighton, respectively, definitely indicated their sexuality was maybe a bit more *not straight* than they claimed.

But it really wasn't my place.

Jett and Leighton were for sure messing around. The whole apartment knew that. Even if we couldn't see it in the way they interacted, we could definitely *hear* it. And damn, if what they were getting up to didn't have me longing for what I didn't have.

But in reality, while I wanted sex, what I longed for the most was just closeness.

A connection.

Intimacy on an emotional level.

And if sex came from that, all the better.

My thoughts returning to Jett and Leighton, I wasn't sure if they'd put a label on whatever was going on or if Jett had decided on what label worked for himself. And that was completely okay.

I had a feeling Dean was maybe questioning, but I wasn't sure he'd ever admit anything to himself—mainly because he probably thought he risked losing Lucas. Which was dumb because anyone could see Lucas was in love with his best friend—but I suspected Lucas also wasn't making a move in fear of losing Dean.

Anyway, back to living and working on Cravenwood Block.

I loved it.

My job was a bit overwhelming.

Not because I wasn't capable or enjoying it—it really was a nice place to work—but because I quickly realized why the three people before me quit.

The individual who had been in charge of the front desk for several years before retiring had a pretty particular way of doing things. It worked for her, but it was an absolutely terrible way of doing things.

Because she'd always gotten things done and never made mistakes, the bosses let her do it her way. But I had already sat down with the person in charge and asked if I could implement the same system being used in the rest of the health center—and the Midtown hospital nearby—to ease the confusion and the redundancy of the current methods.

When I'd started in the position, I was handed a thick, worn notebook and a binder with tabbed pages. Years of notes and directions had been scribbled, typed, and sticky-noted on ripped, stained, smudged pages.

I'd almost cried, but I figured it was a time for me to show what I was made of. I'd dived right in and ended up pretty quickly making heads and tails of the mess, but I'd also demanded a meeting with my boss to request changes—backed up by sound reasons, evidence, and simple solutions.

Dean said everyone was thrilled with the change because now everything would match up. Really, the lady in my spot wasn't in the wrong—she'd set up her own little system long before they'd implemented the center-wide programs—but she should have been forced to convert to the new way instead of being allowed to keep going. In the long run, it would have saved her a shit-load of time and energy.

And now, I was saving myself all of that time and energy.

"You have the weekend off?" Ollie asked me as I fixed water for my hot chocolate and poured a bowl of cereal. I'd ventured to the cute little Cravenwood grocery store and picked up a few essentials, although I needed to go to a discount type place to get the majority of my groceries and toiletries.

"I work today, but I'm off tomorrow," I said.

Julian walked into the kitchen and I nearly swallowed my tongue. Most everyone in the apartment walked around in their underwear. It didn't bother me. I definitely wasn't a prude, but I usually stuck to shorts or lounge pants. Leighton and Lucas would parade through in just skimpy pairs I'd barely call underwear. Everyone else mostly wore boxers or boxer briefs.

Ollie in his underwear didn't unnerve me.

Leighton in his bikinis barely made me bat an eye.

Lucas was attractive, but I wasn't panting over him.

Bash, Dean, and Jett were hot, but they didn't really turn my head.

Julian in his boxers? Damn near had me melting into a pile of quivering goo.

Ollie knew it, too, if the smirk on his face was anything to go by.

Leighton was likely too busy trying to get Jett's attention.

Luckily, Julian didn't seem to notice my drool and the way my eyes were glued to him.

"I'm heading over to the mall and the big grocery store tomorrow if you want to go and get a few things," Julian said.

"Oh! I need to—" Ollie snapped his mouth shut and grinned at his brother. "Ya know what, never mind. I actually have...stuff I need to do tomorrow." He grabbed his chocolate milk and toast and made his way to the living room to plop down next to Bash.

Julian stepped closer. "Did you want to go with me tomorrow? I could show you around, you could get stocked up. Make a day of it?" He seemed hesitant, almost as if he wasn't sure spending the day with him was something I'd want to do.

Honestly, I likely would have been touched and down for a day together whether it had been Julian or any of the guys. The fact it had been Julian to offer his time to me made my heart flutter and warning sirens go off in my head. I'd gotten way too wrapped up in this man from the first moment I'd met him. None of it was his fault—Julian was just gorgeous, kind, and caring which seemed to be my kryptonite.

No one since my mom had ever wanted to spend their time with me unless it was getting them something in return. Although, I guess my first foster parents devoted themselves to me—I was young and barely surviving trauma when they were ripped away too, so I didn't have a lot of concrete memories of them.

And now Julian wanted to spend his day off with me?

Show me around? Make sure I got to the stores where my money would go the furthest?

The best thing about it was Julian wasn't offering in order to gain favor or get me to do something in return. He was just a genuinely kind, helpful person.

And my big fat crush grew exponentially every damn day.

I should have said no.

I should have told him I was busy.

Instead, I smiled. "Yeah, that sounds good."

Tomorrow couldn't come soon enough.

———

"You okay with the mall first? Figure we'll end up with some cold items at the store. We can put them in the cooler in the trunk, but it's probably best to make that one of our last stops," Julian said as he maneuvered the truck into a parking space at the mall the next morning.

"Yeah, that makes sense."

"You have anything in particular you might need here?" Julian asked.

"I'll look at the scrub shop and see if they've got anything on sale." I wasn't very familiar with Midtown, but I'd looked up the local mall so I'd know what stores were available. "I'm making it fine on the two sets the center gave me, but having two or three other pairs would make it easier."

We made our way to the entrance. The place wasn't yet busy, but the scent of cinnamon floated on the air indicating the day was just starting for the shops inside.

"Damn, don't tell Leighton, but we're cheating on him today." Julian gestured toward a little corner shop called Sinful Cinnamon Rolls. "This is why I told you not to eat breakfast. Grab that corner table and I'll order. You want hot chocolate?"

"Orange juice, please." I'd enjoyed a hot chocolate at home and knew the roll plus another sweet drink would be too much. Reaching into my backpack for money, I stopped, cheeks flushing, when Julian waved me off.

"My treat. Save our table."

Our table.

How did something as mundane as the man saying to save a table make my heart pitter-patter? Was I truly that starved for people treating me nicely?

In a way, yes.

But it wasn't like my life had been void of interaction.

I'd had classmates, teachers, work acquaintances.

It was the way Julian made me feel like his time and attention were all for me.

That was what had me all aflutter.

And that was dangerous.

Julian likely saw me as nothing more than a down-on-his luck kid.

There was no way he'd find me sexually or romantically attractive.

Right?

"Here we go," Julian said as he placed an orange juice in front of me before setting a plate down with the most gigantic cinnamon roll I'd ever seen. "This is why I needed you with me. Can't have me clogging up my arteries by eating a whole one." He winked and sat down with his coffee. Handing me a fork, he used a knife to section the roll into quarters. "Dig in."

"This is insanely huge," I said, unable to hide my smile as we both forked up bites of the ooey-gooey cinnamon roll.

"And insanely delicious."

We ate in silence for a bit, but it was comfortable. I liked being with Julian. He had a calming presence and I never felt on-edge around him. Well, maybe my somewhat latent libido experienced some tension, but it wasn't unwelcome. He'd quickly become a safe-space for me—even if he was unaware of that position.

"So, I couldn't help but notice the books you put on your desk," Julian said.

"It's so perfect with its little bookshelf," I replied. I'd been so thrilled to have a home for my treasured books. "And I've got plenty of room for more now that I'm not toting them around."

"You like to read?"

"Pretty much as much as I like to breathe," I answered, my chest getting all warm and tight when I thought of escaping into books.

"We'll hit the bookstore, and I can take you to the library on the way home. You can get a card and check out as many books as you want. It's not *on* Cravenwood Block, but it's a short enough walk."

I could only blink, my heart and brain short-circuiting.

Did this big, somewhat rough-looking, soft-spoken, gorgeous man just refer to our place as *home*, offer to take me to a bookstore, *and* tell me he'd help me get a library card?

That's it.

I was gone.

Hook, line, and sinker.

He had my heart.

Maybe he'd never know it, but I was ruined for anyone else.

Julian would go off and find himself a man his age to settle down with.

I'd maybe eventually accept an underwhelming relationship with a man who at least didn't hurt me.

We'd go our separate ways with only fond memories.

But no one would ever replace Julian in my heart.

It just wouldn't happen.

Fate had brought us together—two perfect halves of a whole—and I wanted to savor the fanciful hope and swoony, fluttering feeling he gave me for as long as possible.

"That sounds perfect." I took a bite of cinnamon roll, followed by a swallow of juice. "Just a warning, you'll likely have to drag me out of the bookstore, I can get a bit caught up and forget the time."

"Not a problem," he answered with a smile.

We finished our breakfast and threw away our trash before making our way toward one of the stores I wanted to visit.

Julian took a seat outside the scrub shop so he could check his work email. "Don't rush, I'm not in a hurry."

The health center policy stated I either needed to wear scrubs in navy blue or business casual attire. Since any money I had for everyday type clothing would be going to pieces that weren't focused on business casual, I'd decided to do just scrubs at work. They were easy, comfortable, and I liked the uniform feel of dressing like the rest of the staff.

I lucked out and found three pairs of scrubs in my size on the clearance rack. Beaming as I clutched my purchase to my chest, I made my way toward Julian.

"Where to?" he asked.

"I don't have anywhere I *need* to go."

"Let's head to the bookstore," Julian said.

On our way, we passed a men's store with work clothes.

"Those shirts make me think of you," I said, nodding toward the various shades of denim shirts and plaid flannels.

Julian smiled. "I *may* get most of my clothes there. Ollie says I'm the only guy he knows who can make a denim work shirt look good." His cheeks flushed. "Not that I think I look good in them, they're just easy for my job."

Without thinking, I bumped my shoulder into his. "He's not wrong, you *do* look good in the denim. And no one should look as good in carpenter jeans as you do." Now it was my turn to flush.

"They're a statement I guess," Julian said with a chuckle. "I don't wear them for fashion, they're just easy and fit with my job."

"I like that one with the pearl buttons," I said, pointing to a shirt in the window. "That darker denim color would go well with the khaki carpenter pants you've got."

"Think so?" Julian asked, contemplating the shirt.

"Definitely. My past may be all kinds of fucked up, but I know what looks good." I gestured toward the store. "Let's go in."

Julian found the darker denim shirt with pearl buttons in his size and took it from the rack. "Anything else you think would look good?"

"That gray button-up would be good with dark-wash jeans if you ever need to dress up for an evening. And that black button-up would look good with a dark gray chino if you've got them."

"Dress up? Like for a date?" Julian asked, cocking his brow.

My cheeks heated. "Or a meeting or just dinner with the guys. I'm not exactly an expert on *dating*, but I can tell you what would look good if you need to spiff up."

Julian's eyes bore into mine and I swore there was something close to interest in them. "Good to know. Would you maybe want to change th—"

"Can I help you, gentlemen?" a clerk asked, interrupting whatever Julian had been about to say.

Change? Change what?

Julian found his size in the other two shirts I'd suggested and paid for his purchases. "Okay, definitely time for the bookstore. That's more clothes shopping than I usually do in a year," he joked.

The moment I walked through the doors of the bookstore, I was transported.

The scent of books always did it.

"Oh my god," I said breathlessly.

"What?" Julian asked, seeming concerned.

"I've carried fifteen books around with me over the last several years—all for different reasons—they're the ones you see on my shelf. But I have a wish list of titles I want to buy someday when I'm not toting the books around." I pointed toward a display. "Those two box sets are top on my list."

Julian moved toward the display with me.

Miss Peregrine's Home for Peculiar Children and *Mortal Instruments* were two series I'd devoured as a preteen and teen.

"Get them," Julian said. "You're not living out of a duffel anymore. They'd look great on your shelf. If you need a bigger shelf, I'm sure there's one in the basement."

It was a perfect opening to let him know I knew about the furniture, but Leighton pleading for his balls danced through my head.

"I shouldn't splurge on *both*. I'll get one this time and one next time." I traced fingers over the spines of both book sets. "The *Mortal Instruments* one is on a better sale. I'll get that one this time."

Julian plucked it from the shelf. "I'll carry it while you look around. I'm going to go over there," he pointed to the little café. "I'll do some work and drink a coffee while you browse."

Bringing my dreams of a gorgeous man supporting me in every way to life, Julian gave me a smile and headed toward a table with my books in hand.

An hour later, after I'd forced myself not to buy anything other than the box set, I found Julian and held out my hands for the box. "What did you buy?" I asked, pointing to his large bag.

"Just something for a friend," he answered. "You want to get lunch before groceries? I'm not dying for food yet, but an empty stomach in the ice cream section is dangerous."

"Agreed, sounds good." I headed toward the cashier. "Sorry I took so long."

"Don't worry about it. I got some emails answered, a gift bought, and a good coffee. Not a bad way to spend an hour." He took my bag of scrubs while I checked out. "I'll bring you here anytime you want. I can browse and drink coffee while you lose yourself in the shelves."

As if I needed any other reason to be infatuated with this man.

Julian stuck the clothing bags behind the seat when we reached the truck. I put my bag of books between my feet.

"So, um, I wanted to get you something to welcome you to the apartment," Julian said and shoved the bag he'd been holding my way.

"What? You didn't have to do that."

"Open it." He bit his lip as if nervous.

"Julian," I said, feeling awkward and special all at the same time. I peeked into the bag and gasped. "No, this is too much."

Inside was the box set of *Miss Peregrine's Home for Peculiar Children* and a gift card.

"Didn't want you to miss out on the books. The card is so you can get something next time we come," Julian explained softly.

Surging to cover the space between us, I kissed him on the cheek. "Thank you. That's maybe the nicest thing anyone has ever done for me."

Julian's cheeks pinked and he shrugged. "You saved me

from having a weird roommate and helped me get some fashionable shirts, it's the least I could do."

Cocking a brow, I said, "Coming from someone who already furnished my room when everyone else had to furnish their own, I'm pretty sure it was above and beyond what you needed to do." I placed a hand on his upper arm. "For real, Julian, thank you. You've already done so much for me. I can pay you back."

Julian narrowed his eyes. "No. It wasn't a big deal. Everything but the mattress was just sitting in the basement." He shook his head and mumbled, "Those guys can't keep a secret worth shit."

"I don't know what I did to deserve such a great place to live, roommates I love, and a friend who treats me so well, but thank you." Tears stung my eyes.

"It's really not a big deal," Julian said gruffly as he started the truck.

"It is, at least to me." I hugged the box of books to my chest. "No one has ever done anything so nice for me without expecting something in return."

"No strings or expectations attached, promise," Julian said with a wink. "Maybe you'll tell me about your books someday?" he asked as we drove up to a little deli near the discount store.

"Well, the box set you got me is full of books I read pretty much right after my mom died," I said.

"I'm sorry," Julian said. "I didn't know."

"She died in a car wreck when I was ten. I ended up with a pretty great foster family for a few years, but then the dad was in a terrible wreck, paralyzed, and the mom couldn't keep up with me, my therapy, and his injuries." I lost myself in the grip of how unfair life had been, but shook my head and continued. "The first thing that caught my eye about those books was the title. I felt like a freak at times. I already knew I was different—even though I wouldn't settle on gay until later—and a home was something I'd lost, so a home for peculiar children struck a chord. There are several themes in the stories, but belonging, protection, and family are the ones that spoke to me the most. The series sucked me in and gave me an escape."

"I've never read them," Julian said as we stepped into line at the deli.

"You're welcome to borrow them anytime you'd like," I said, warmth blooming through me when he smiled at my offer.

Once we'd ordered and found a seat with our food, he pressed on. "What about the other books you bought?"

"*Mortal Instruments* is pretty heavy in the family theme as well, but I read those later in my teen years. I read to escape and that series really provided a great fantasy world to travel to—gave me the love and family I craved, bad ass characters and powers, revenge, fights..." I sighed. "So great."

"I think Ollie watched the movie? Or was it a TV series?"

"Both. The books were great. The movie was so-so. I liked the television series—but mainly because I had a thing for Malec."

Julian cocked a brow. "Do tell."

"Alec Lightwood and Magnus Bane—fans shipped them as Malec. I just loved their love story. But I also loved Clary and Jace. And Simon." I sighed again. "I still liked the book series best, but the show was great."

"I kinda wish I'd ever loved a book as much as you seem to love the ones you've read," Julian said with soft smile.

"Nah, I don't love *every* book. It's just not possible. Just like we don't love every food or every movie or every pair of shoes we see, we're not going to love every book. One I love may not be your favorite and vice versa."

"I remember liking *Holes*, *Because of Winn Dixie*, and this book my teacher read to the class called *Among the Hidden*," Julian said.

I nearly choked on my lemonade.

"Oh my god," I murmured. "I loved *Holes* and *Because of Winn Dixie*. But *Among the Hidden*? For real?"

"What? You didn't like that one?"

Grinning, I just shook my head. "I'll tell you more at home."

Julian cocked his head. "Wait, how are you twenty-four and I'm thirty-five and we've read the same books?"

I shrugged. "You read them when they first came out. I read them a decade later when they were considered *classics*," I teased.

"Ouch." Julian rubbed at his chest. "Why don't you just tell me you'll take me to see about rooming with LuLu at the retirement home?"

Laughing, I threw away our trash. "I haven't met her yet, but from what Ollie says, she's a hoot. I'm sure she'd make a great roommate."

"Let's go get groceries before I need to get home for my nap and afternoon heart medication—you know, since I'm a *classic*."

I bumped his hip. "You know I'm just joking, right? Those books were only ten or so years old when I read them. You're nowhere near *old*."

We piled into the truck and headed toward our last stop of the day.

By the time we'd selected all of our groceries and separated out what we'd share the cost of and what we'd pay for on our own, I was seriously dragging and my cheeks hurt from smiling so much.

"Library?" Julian asked as we neared Cravenwood.

"I don't have anything with my name and address on it

yet," I said, wrinkling my nose. "I doubt they'll give me a card."

He held up a finger as if telling me to wait a moment and reached across me to the glove compartment.

The scent of soap and shampoo tickled my nose and I fought the urge to breathe him in. His heat, so close, had my heart thumping.

"Thought about that and grabbed this from the junk mail pile on our table. I think yours got mixed in with mine or Dean's, but this might work." He slammed the glove compartment shut and handed me an envelope with my name and address on it. "If not, I'll be sure my info is updated and you can use mine until you can get your own. How's that?"

I truly wasn't sure how to keep from melting over this man.

"Perfect. Thanks."

Thirty minutes later, I had my own library card, a complimentary tote bag, and six books borrowed.

Julian pulled the truck around to the back of the apartment complex and unlocked the delivery door to push a cart outside.

"Dang, I'm definitely going grocery shopping with you every time. I was dreading hauling all this shit inside and you just solved the entire problem."

Julian smirked. "What's the point of having perks with a job if you don't take advantage of them?"

"Ohhh, people are going to give us the evil eye on the elevator—taking up all the room and using apartment things to our own gain," I whispered.

"Nah, we're using the freight elevator. No one even has to know."

"I like the way you think."

We unloaded our groceries and Julian took the cart back downstairs with plans to move his truck into a parking spot.

When he returned, I had my two new book sets stored on the shelving unit of my desk.

"Everything good?" Julian asked from my doorway.

"Yeah, come see." I gestured him in and immediately loved the way he looked in my room. How this man had so quickly and completely become a friend, someone I looked forward to spending time with, I didn't know or even begin to comprehend. I'd never really had the chance to build deeper connections with people, even if I'd felt any kind of tug toward them in the past. And the spark between Julian and me was more than just my physical attraction to him— more than just my very possible daddy issues and desperate need for a father-type person in my life.

I liked him.

Liked listening to him talk.

Liked being around him.

Liked making him laugh.

The situation was new and strange for me, but I didn't hate it.

Not at all.

I just hoped it didn't end up getting me in trouble.

"Hey, that's the book I was talking about," Julian said, reaching for *Among the Hidden* on my shelf. "There's a whole series? Oh, wow."

"That's what I was going to tell you," I said. "That series is seven books and it's one I carried around all this time. I absolutely adored it. My teacher was reading the second book to my class when I lost my foster parents. I'm sure it was a coping mechanism, but I made it a mission to read the entire series. Family and friendship have always been themes I'm a sucker for, but this series also had freedom and courage. Luke having courage was something that kept me going. The quest for freedom and escaping a bad situation was sometimes the only thing that got me through the shit years with the new foster family."

Julian traced his fingers over the spines of the seven books. "What happened? With the new one?" His soft words went straight to my heart. "You don't have to tell me…"

"No, it's okay." I'd never really told many people about my past, but I wanted to share with Julian. "After my foster dad got hurt, the family I ended up with wasn't the greatest. The dad was a pastor at the local church and he was mean. The mom did nothing about it because if he was beating me he wasn't hurting her or her kids. He used to beat a Bible story into me pretty much every morning—I was a quiet kid, always trying to just blend in and get by—especially after my mom died—but I'm sure by that point, people were well-aware I was different—even though I'd never come out and told anyone I was gay." I stared at the wall, distancing myself from the painful memories. "If he'd gotten too into it and left marks I couldn't hide under clothing, he'd have my foster mom call me in sick to school or pull me out and homeschool me for a while. He moved me from the public school to the private church school 'to keep those damn nosy teachers from butting into our business.' He'd hit me and then take me to the walk-in clinic a few days later—bitching the whole time about what a pussy I was. For the first year, it seemed there was always a different person running the front desk. Then a new lady started working there. She saw me once or twice, then she wasn't there a few times, but then she saw me like four times in a row. She pissed the pastor off when she insisted he sit in the waiting room instead of going back with me—he always wanted to be right there while the nurse or doctor checked me over. It was a small town and they were like a rotating door with employees—I always wondered who he had in his pocket for no one to notice the number of times

I was brought in. But this lady, she noticed and she wasn't scared of him like so many others. While he was ranting and raving, she filled the doctor in and called the department of child services. I was removed and he was arrested." I shrugged. "That was when I was fifteen. It sucked to be that age and bounced from one home to the next until I was eighteen, but at least the abuse stopped."

"What did you do once you turned eighteen?" Julian asked.

I swallowed thickly. "I survived and made it to this point. That's all that matters." I didn't regret those decisions. I'd very likely make the same choices all over again if I had to, but I wanted to leave it in the past. "Fresh start and all that."

Maybe one day, I'd share the story with Julian.

But I wasn't ready.

Not yet.

"I'm sorry you had to go through that," Julian said, putting his arm around me and pulling me into a hug.

My entire world shifted.

Nothing had ever felt as right as being in Julian's arms.

My mom had been a hugger.

My first foster parents were very affectionate.

But hugs weren't something I got a lot of after they had to give me up.

Definitely not from the pastor.

Hell, I wasn't ever in any foster home long enough to even feel comfortable with hugs after that.

And from eighteen until I made my way to Cravenwood Block, I didn't trust anyone enough to allow hugs. Yeah, I'd touched and been touched, but not in the comfortable, caring way of Julian's hug.

The one boyfriend I'd had a couple years ago would have pissed himself laughing if I'd told him I wanted a hug. He had expectations for me—based on information he enjoyed holding over me as a threat—and he made it clear I was his sex toy and nothing more.

Hindsight was definitely twenty-twenty.

I didn't regret the way I survived back then, but I did regret letting that asshole control me and use me.

I'd wanted to keep the information he was holding over me tucked away, especially since he was threatening to tell my employer, but I should have left him sooner and never looked back.

I'd finally smartened up and done the right thing, but I'd wasted way too much time with that man.

When I would have stayed tucked against Julian forever, he cleared his throat and pulled away. "Sorry, I'm a hugger. Just tell me to knock it off if it bothers you."

"It doesn't bother me," I murmured.

The air between us mixed with awkwardness and tension.

"Tell me about the other books."

I took his bait. "Well, they all have special places in my heart for one reason or another." I took a beat-up board book from the shelf. "*Goodnight Moon* was a favorite when I was little. My mom read it to me from the time I was born. When the state people came to take me to my first foster family, they told me I could take some books. I grabbed *Goodnight Moon* first." I ran my fingers over the cover. "I also took *Love You Forever*," I said, pointing to the book. "It always made my mom cry to read it, but I wanted it with me as a reminder we'd always love each other, even though she was gone." I took a deep breath. "And *Oh, the Places You'll Go* was the other one I took that first time. Mom had gotten the book for me when I started Kindergarten. She sent it in every year for my teachers to sign. The original plan was to have teachers from Kindergarten through twelfth grade sign it. She died at the end of my fourth-grade year and the plan died along with her. But I like looking at the message from my mom—she wrote it the summer before I started school—and the five teachers who *did* get to jot little messages. Sometimes I wish I'd kept up with asking teachers to sign it, but there were a lot of times I wasn't at a school for very long, so many of my teachers didn't really know me."

"God, Shaw," Julian mumbled. He put his arm around me again, tucking me close to his side.

"I'm not telling you this for pity," I said.

"And I'm not pitying you. You're fucking amazing. It's not pity, it's more like awe." He pointed toward another book. "What about that one?"

"*The Boxcar Children*," I said with a smile, barely able to breathe for fear Julian would move his arm from around me. "My first foster family picked up on the fact I liked to read and they helped me pick out some books at the library. I was a huge fan of *Hatchet*, *My Side of the Mountain*, and that one." I pointed to the book about children who lived in an abandoned train car. "It was a super easy read, but I liked the kids and the story. I used to imagine being brave enough and strong enough to survive on my own like those characters."

"And you did," Julian answered gruffly.

I smiled, tears pricking my eyes. "Yeah, I guess I did."

"*Perks of Being a Wallflower*?" Julian pulled the book from the shelf. "I thought that was just a movie."

I sighed and pretended to be put out. "No, the movie was based on the book. That book was the first I ever read with gay characters. They weren't the *main* part of the story, but I remember my heart beating faster when I read about them. I read a lot of fiction with queer characters now, but back then, when I was still navigating high school and just trying to survive, that book was like a beacon of hope for me." I took the book from his hands and flipped through the pages. "Charlie is a bit odd and I felt a connection to him."

"You think you're odd?"

I shrugged. "Aren't we all kinda odd in our own ways? I used to want to be nothing but the most normal guy ever. But as I've gotten older, I've realized I just want to be me. Even if it means being a bit different."

"Makes sense. I fought through all that trying to be normal stuff, until I realized someone else's normal wasn't mine and I just had to be true to myself. Once I accepted what *my* normal was, I was a lot happier." Julian cocked his head. "The Bible?"

I chuckled. "Sure, why not?"

Julian gazed down at me. "Guess I thought after the pastor you maybe didn't want anything to do with religion."

"What are your thoughts on religion?" I asked, stalling. What would Julian think of the reason why I had the Bible in my collection?

Julian shrugged. "Organized religion isn't my thing. I guess I'd say I'm more spiritual than religious. You?"

"I stole it from the pastor," I said with a soft snort. "It was the Bible he'd read from every morning when he'd force me to listen to his lessons—and usually smacked me around if I was lucky, beat the shit out of me if it was a bad day—so when the cops took him, and his wife stormed out of the house, I slipped it in my bag before the department people came to move me. Again. I guess I figured if he didn't have that damn book, maybe he couldn't hurt anyone else." I shook my head. "But the book wasn't the problem, the evil was in him."

We were quiet for a bit, Julian keeping his arm around me.

"Serves the bastard right," Julian finally said. "What other books do you want to get?" he asked, moving from the heavier topic.

"I devoured *The Magic Treehouse* series when I was little, so I'd get that as a good memory of happier times. We did a book study on *A Wrinkle in Time* and I really liked that story. And as much as I can't stand the author, the Harry Potter stories were near and dear to my heart and got me through some really hard times."

Julian nodded. "Yeah, that series has always been so controversial. I remember all the Bible thumpers freaking out about it being witchcraft and evil. And now it's tainted by finding out the author is a transphobe. The stories were good, though."

"For me, I loved the stories, but it was more just the ability to disappear in a good book, a different world."

"Did you ever read *From the Mixed-up Files of Mrs. Basil E. Frankweiler*? I remember liking that one," Julian mused.

"Kids hiding in a museum? I remember it vaguely. I think a teacher read it maybe in fifth grade." I yawned.

"Sorry, I've been hogging your time." Julian moved away from me and I immediately missed the warm press of his arm.

"Thank you for today," I said, biting my lip and catching his eye. "Honestly, this was probably the best day I've had since before my mom died. Thank you."

"Any time," Julian answered, his words gruff. He looked as if he wanted to say more, but he shook his head and turned to leave.

I showered, brushed my teeth, and spent the next several hours reading in bed.

When I put the book aside and cuddled up under my blankets, I couldn't help the smile on my face. It had been a damn near perfect day.

That great feeling was tainted overnight when I woke up screaming.

Talking about my past had stirred things up and the nightmare slammed into me.

I wasn't a stranger to the bad dreams, but I hadn't yet had

one in my new home, so I'd hoped maybe the new location was a fresh start and the nightmares hadn't followed me.

I'd been wrong.

Julian stuck his head into my room as I shuddered and wiped tears from my face.

"You okay?" he asked, making his way toward my bed.

"Yeah, just a nightmare," I answered, my words shaky and weak.

He sat on the edge of my bed—had he been anyone from my past, I likely would have felt uncomfortable, but with Julian, I just wanted to throw myself into his arms. "Want me to sit for a bit?"

"You don't have to," I hedged, fighting the urge to cuddle against him.

"Ollie used to have bad dreams when he first came to live with Dad and me, I don't mind." Julian shifted to lean against my headboard, tucking me against his side. "This okay?"

I nodded against him, not even letting myself question how I felt so completely safe and comfortable around him.

"You want to talk about it?"

"Nah, it's always just a sad and scary mix of my mom dying, the pastor, and some other junk. It's not petrifying, but it's no fun to be jerked from sleep screaming, sweating, and your heart going a million miles a minute."

"Wanna talk or try to go back to sleep?"

"Won't sleep for a bit," I answered. Despite being tired, the dreams always shook me up too much to sleep for a while.

We were quiet for a while.

"Tell me about your tattoos," Julian eventually said.

I hesitated briefly, but launched into a description of them. "I've always liked tattoos and will probably get more—doesn't hurt to have Jett living here—but these were all paid for by a former boss."

"Your boss made you get tattooed?" Julian's voice was strained like he was holding back anger.

"Thought it would help on the job," I said, knowing I was being vague. "But he paid for them and I like ink anyway, so I went with it."

"Did you get to pick what you got?"

"Yeah. Honestly, I went with some pretty generic things. The dragon design on my shoulder was first. Then we added the flowers down my arm. The old-fashioned pocket watch on my chest was the last one before I left that job."

"Next one you get should be for you and only you," Julian said gruffly.

"Yeah," I said around a yawn. "Maybe I'll chat with Jett about ideas."

"You ready to sleep?"

I wanted to ask him to stay.

Wanted to spend hours in his arms just talking.

Just *being*.

I'm not sure I'd ever felt so safe and allowed to just *be* as I did with Julian.

"Yeah, probably better try to get a few hours. Alarm is going to go off early." I yawned again, knowing I'd fall asleep pretty quickly thanks to the decompression time Julian had given me.

"Okay," Julian said as he stood from the bed and stretched. "Holler if you need anything."

And then I was alone in the dark room.

With the remnants of a nightmare and the warm scent of a man.

Only one of those was going to be allowed to dance through my dreams until morning.

When I woke to a very obnoxious alarm what seemed like only moments later, I couldn't help but smile. I could still smell Julian on my bed. Still feel his comforting warmth pressed against me.

Yeah, the guy was likely just treating me the way he would have treated his little brother, but the feelings I was having for him were anything but brotherly.

I hadn't come to Cravenwood Block for a relationship.

I wasn't under any false hope Julian would actually have any interest in me.

But damn, the man was definite fodder for the imagination and the exact mix of masculine, caring protection I'd longed for my entire life.

Pulling up my email, I promised myself I'd waste no more than five minutes checking messages before I hopped into the shower.

I had an early shift and needed to get ready if I was going to have time to stop by Cravin'-a-Cup to get hot chocolate.

The email subject line caught me off-guard and nearly sent me spiraling.

I'm Watching and Soon They Will Be Too from a Gmail address of BooIFoundYou.

My heart nearly pounded out of my chest as I clicked on the message.

You thought you could run away, but I found you. All those new friends you're making will soon know the dirty truth about you. This should be fun. Now you can pay for ruining everything.

Shit.

Fuck.

What the hell was happening?

The embedded video started playing and I knew immediately what it was.

One of my scenes.

One of my *many* scenes.

Not my earlier ones, but one from my second production company.

My first adult film producer had been a good guy—he'd been small potatoes compared to the huge studios, but everything was pretty much above-board.

I'd hated the films, but I'd made good money and Benny had treated me well. Unfortunately, Benny's company got shut down when two of his talents overdosed. He promised he'd start up again, but I needed the money and couldn't wait around.

The second producer had a bigger, flashier company and was one of the meanest assholes I'd ever met. While I'd hated most every moment of my early film career, I despised *and* feared every moment of my later years in the adult film industry. The producer, Luka, had been let go from several of the bigger, more popular companies because of his penchant for mixing creepy and angry into his interactions with the actors.

Luka had threatened me and beat the shit out of me when I left his company—and the industry all together—at age twenty-two. I'd survived from eighteen to twenty-one with Benny, but even just a year with Luka had been more than I could handle. I'd lucked out with Benny even though he wasn't one of the top companies. Luka had been bad news from the very beginning. His methods and videos screamed sketchy and his fists proved to me I needed to get out if I wanted to keep myself alive and well.

After healing from the beating, I skipped town—fearful for my life because Luka was an addict and pure evil and he'd told me he'd never stop until he found me and got my "sweet, money-making ass" back in front of the camera or killed me.

With the money I'd saved up thanks to the films—I'd thrifted it away and lived beyond modestly in order to have a nest egg—I was able to get a small studio apartment. The place was shit, but it allowed me to save most of my money and start a job in a hospital kitchen far away from Luka and my old life.

From twenty-two until not too long ago, I took classes, worked in the kitchen, and dated one of the cooks. Max had seen my films, recognized me, and asked me out. I didn't *like* him, but I liked the attention.

When I let him know I wasn't really feeling it a few months later, he freaked out. Threatened to show the films to the hospital so I'd lose my job. Threatened to send the films to my teachers.

So, I stayed with him until I finished getting the data entry certification.

He didn't *abuse* me in as far as he wasn't like the pastor or Luka.

But Max liked his sex rough and his partners meek.

I survived his threats and being his fuck toy until I finished classes.

And then I split.

Max texted me before I got rid of my old phone and told me he'd track me down. *I'll find you. You better keep an eye out for me.*

Was the email from Luka or Max?

It didn't feel like Benny—hell, that guy was old enough, he may have died from lung cancer after nearly seventy years of chain-smoking cigars.

Max had links to my videos.

Luka did as well.

Both of them were mean and manipulative.

Both had threatened to find me.

Max had only lost a sex object—truly, I was likely one of several for him.

Luka had lost money when I left.

I knew I brought in a lot of revenue for him.

Even though I'd hated making the films—and

paradoxically would forever be grateful because the job had allowed me to eventually get to this point in my life—I'd been one of the top stars and money-makers for both Benny and Luka.

My gut told me Luka was behind the email.

And he knew about my new roommates.

How?

It wasn't like I'd ditched my old identity, but I thought I'd flown far enough under the radar to avoid my past catching up with me.

Fear clawed its way up my throat and I let loose a strangled raw cry tinged with terrified frustration.

Hadn't I dealt with enough?

Hadn't I worked hard enough to overcome?

Why now?

Why here?

Why *me*?

Should I just leave?

Tell the guys and ask for help?

Could I deal with them knowing about the films?

I wasn't ashamed of the way I'd survived those five years.

But I didn't want my new friends to know.

I wanted a chance to start over.

A fresh beginning, damn it.

I moved the email message to a private folder and climbed out of bed.

I had to get to work.

Maybe I'd figure something out later.

Maybe I'd ask for help.

Hell, maybe I'd call Luka's bluff.

What was the worst that could happen?

FOUR

Julian

I WAS ALREADY AWAKE when I heard Shaw's alarm going off.

Sleep had eluded me all night.

It had taken every ounce of conviction to leave Shaw's room after his nightmare.

But what the hell was I going to do? Ravish the kid in his own bed after he'd woken up terrified?

Right.

It was bad enough I'd crawled into bed with him after having my arm around him more than once earlier in the day.

Once back in my own bed, I'd spent the rest of the night questioning myself, berating my actions, wondering what the hell had gotten into me.

I was a caretaker.

A protector.

It was just my nature.

But I usually showed that through offering my truck, helping a person find an apartment, cooking dinner, or loaning money.

While I *was* a hugger—at least more so than maybe Jett or

Bash, maybe not as much as Leighton—I didn't usually go around pulling the guys close to me, hugging them, or tucking them under my arm.

If Ollie had a bad dream, I'd definitely go into his room to check on him.

But Leighton? Lucas? Dean?

I'd likely knock on the door and ask if everything was okay.

Not go sit on their bed and gather them under my arm.

But reaching for Shaw was easy and natural.

And he seemed to be okay with it.

In fact, he seemed to take comfort in it.

Which wasn't surprising after the shit history he'd endured.

I wasn't a violent man by nature, but I wanted to find the pastor and give him a taste of his own medicine. Or turn Ollie and Leighton loose on him.

Was Shaw's comfort in my arms a reciprocated attraction? Or just his desperate need for a father-type figure in his life.

As we got closer, was I misreading his cues?

Were the smiles, looks, and conversations just Shaw's desire for a close, comforting relationship with a male?

Or were the vibes I thought I was picking up actually signs of the same attraction I felt toward him?

I ran a hand over my face.

What the hell was I doing being attracted to a much younger tenant? And which was worse? The fact he was a tenant and roommate? Or the fact he was so much younger?

Sure, eleven years wasn't a lifetime, but I worried about looking like I was taking advantage of him. I'd never really considered myself to have a *type*, but I'd usually dated men right around my own age if and when I actually dated.

The kid was all up in my head—or, I was all up in my

head over him—and I wasn't sure what to do with all the thoughts and feelings.

"Morning," I said as I met up with Shaw in the kitchen. He looked completely edible in his navy scrubs—the short sleeves showing off his sinewy arms and the slim-fit pants accenting his long legs and narrow waist. While some people allowed themselves to be engulfed by big, baggy scrubs, Shaw had done a great job choosing the perfect size for his build.

His eyes showed lack of sleep and he seemed tense. "Morning," he mumbled, clearly preoccupied.

"You wanna make pizza with me for dinner tonight?" I asked, referring to the ingredients we'd gotten at the store.

He blinked at me as if pulling himself from wherever his head had traveled to. "Oh, um, yeah. That sounds good."

"You grabbing hot chocolate before work?" I asked.

"Mmhm," he hummed. "Should have time."

"Want a walking partner?" Maybe I should have picked up on his clues and left him alone, but my days didn't seem complete without the Shaw-time I'd grown accustomed to during the short time we'd been living together. "I could use some coffee, didn't sleep worth shit."

His face filled with regret. "I'm sorry I woke you. Next time, just ignore me. I'm used to the dreams; can take care of myself," he mumbled.

"Nah, I didn't mind. Just because you *can* doesn't mean you should have to. It wasn't a problem. Just my own stupid head couldn't shut itself off once I went back to bed." I grabbed my phone and keys. "Ready?"

He hadn't actually said he wanted me to walk with him, but he smiled like he didn't mind. "Yeah. I'll get Dean a coffee too—he's on the early shift."

Cravenwood Block was waking up and welcoming the day as we made our way to Cravin'-a-Cup.

"Hey, don't forget we're having our Nacho Night. You're

coming, right?" Leighton, Ollie, and I had used the rooftop before the rest of the guys moved in, but having all eight of us up there seemed picture perfect.

The way the eight of us had all come together as great friends in such a short amount of time made me happier than I ever would have thought.

Knowing I had my dad, Ollie, and a great group of friends just made my days more enjoyable.

"What?" Shaw scowled. "Oh, um, yeah, I'll try to be there."

"We picked a night the health center isn't open so you and Dean are free. Lucas asked off. Jett isn't taking appointments after six that day. And Leighton worked his schedule to fit. You've *got* to be there. Please?" Part of me wanted Shaw to realize how important to our little group he was. The selfish part of me just wanted him around.

He smiled, but his eyes showed me he was a million miles away. "You guys don't need me there to eat nachos. If I'm not around, I'm sure you'll survive."

"Nope. The party only goes on if all of us are there." I bumped my elbow into his. "I know most of you all moved in kinda around the same time and could easily claim to still be virtually strangers, but it feels like our whole little group gelled really well. Maybe you don't have a lot of experience with being part of a group of friends, but I'm telling you now, we want you there."

Shaw's face brightened. "That's nice to hear. I'm hoping I'll be here," he mumbled.

"Be here? Like, be home?" I paused and gently grasped his elbow. "You're being vague and you're entitled to keep things private, but why does it sound like you're hinting you won't even be around?" A weird panic filled my gut. He just moved in. His financial history indicated he'd be able to afford the rent, so I didn't think that was the issue. Why would Shaw be acting as if he was moving out?

"Is it the rent? Can we help in some way?" I asked. "The job is still going well?"

Shaw sighed. "Rent isn't a problem—luckily I saved up a lot before coming here. The job is great, I truly do love it."

I narrowed my eyes. "Is it something we can help with?" Stepping closer, I brushed a chunk of dark hair from his eyes. "You've got a house full of friends willing to help, don't try to do things on your own. Not saying you have to tell us every facet of your life, but we're here."

Shaw closed his eyes for a moment. They were bright with threatening tears when he reopened them. "I'm going to do what's in my power to be here and be at the party. Promise," he said, offering me a watery smile. "Come on, I've got to get my drinks ordered or I'll be late and there will be a line of grumpy patients saying nasty things to me as I open the doors."

I didn't like his vague response as it left me with more questions than answers, but he was a grown man and I couldn't force him to tell me what was going on.

Maybe the dream had fucked him up more than he was letting on.

Shaw needed to get used to the fact he was wanted.

Wanted as a friend and roommate.

Wanted as an employee.

And as fucked up as it made me feel, wanted by me.

In whatever capacity I could get him.

When we walked out of Cravin'-a-Cup, I sipped my coffee and fell into step beside Shaw.

"You're going the wrong way," he said with the first real smile I'd seen all morning.

"Nah, getting my exercise in. When you're at my

advanced age, you really have to be aware of your physical activity," I said, giving him a wink.

Shaw chuckled before taking a drink of his hot chocolate.

We made idle small-talk and before long we'd arrived at the health center.

Dean eyed us both up and down with a gleam in his eye, meeting us at the employee entrance. "Good morning," he said, cheeks flushed as if he'd run most of the way. "Shaw, please tell me that cup is a coffee for me and I'll love you forever."

"It's a coffee for you," Shaw answered. "Figured you'd be running late."

"Figured, huh?" Dean asked, sighing as the coffee touched his tongue.

"For a doctor who is very precise about a lot of things, you have a really bad habit of being late." Shaw shrugged and winked. "It's something I noticed about you early-on. It's slightly annoying, yet somewhat endearing. You and Lucas are so similar, yet so very different. He's so laid back about most things, but a stickler for time. You keep tight control on a lot of stuff, but can't get somewhere on time to save your soul—unless Lucas is getting you there."

Dean's cheeks flushed pinker. "Lucas just likes to be on time so he doesn't miss anything. He's too nosy for his own damn good."

Not for the first time, I wondered about their relationship.

Best friends from childhood, I knew that much.

They'd both brought a date or two around since moving in. It was interesting they always seemed to go out on double-dates. And, though the eight of us hadn't known each other long, six of us had picked up on the fact the double-dates had yet to ever turn into second dates.

Lucas and Dean were interesting for sure.

"We're fixing pizza at home tonight, if you want to join us," I told Dean.

"Sounds good. We'll be there." That was another thing. Lucas and Dean were a package deal ninety-nine percent of the time. Where one was, you'd find the other. Kinda like the saying *Where there's smoke, there's fire*. Lucas and Dean were attached at the hip and it seemed the most natural thing in the world.

I truly did wonder when one or both of them would realize they were pretty much a couple in every sense of the word outside of a sexual relationship.

But it really wasn't my place.

They'd need to figure their shit out on their own. Maybe they'd already addressed it and decided friendship was their best bet.

God knew I had enough of my own shit to deal with without playing matchmaker to two grown men.

Dean gave a wave as he took another grateful sip of his coffee and headed inside.

"Thanks for walking with me. And thanks again for last night." Shaw shifted from foot to foot. "I better get inside."

"Pizza for dinner," I said, pointing at him. "Be there."

He nodded. "Will do. See you then."

———

A COUPLE WEEKS LATER, as we geared up for our Nacho Night, I was no surer of what the heck was going on between Shaw and me.

I'd gotten to know him a lot better—both through casual chats, a few more overnight nightmare recoveries, and just simple observation.

Shaw had a traumatic past—and I had a feeling I only knew a bit of it thanks to what he'd shared with me. My gut told me he'd been through more and the *more* was maybe why he'd seemed distracted and melancholy lately.

His books were his refuge.

He used them as comfort and to escape.

It was nothing to find him curled up with a book at all hours. If he had a day off, he often went to the library and spent hours submerged in his stories either in his bed or the recliner in our living room.

If he was working—which he did a lot, I swear the kid took every spare shift he could. While it may have been for extra money, I got the feeling it was something more. Maybe his way of giving back—trying to be that person to spot the kid in need like the lady who saved him from the pastor. Anyway, if he was working, he had a book with him for breaks, and he often stayed up too late reading before an early shift.

Another thing I'd picked up on was Shaw was uncertain of his place in our group.

Mainly, it appeared to be a trust issue—which was completely understandable with the shit he'd gone through.

In the very beginning, I thought he was maybe scared of some of us, but he'd settled in and gotten more comfortable with all the guys as time had passed. He was just the type who needed time to watch and learn in order to familiarize himself and relax.

He was more comfortable with us now, but it was like he wasn't sure why we wanted him around. He definitely wasn't used to having a group of friends.

What else had I learned?

My attraction and budding feelings for him hadn't waned in the least. In fact, if I was being honest, I wanted him more than ever before.

More than anything, though, I just wanted him in my life.

I wanted to take care of him and protect him—not that I

thought he couldn't do that on his own, but it was where my heart was and I wanted to be the one caring for and protecting him.

If that meant friendship only, I'd deal with it.

If there was a chance for something more, I'd be patient.

I glanced at the gift bag on my dresser.

Was I being ridiculous to get the guy a gift?

I knew the others would give me shit, but buying the items had felt right.

I sighed and peeked into the bag for the third time since packaging it up.

The night we'd made pizza had given me the idea.

Bash had offered to make the pizza sauce from his Aunt LuLu's homemade recipe. We'd all been impressed she made homemade sauce and just as impressed that Bash had the recipe and was willing to make it.

He'd told us LuLu had spent a year hand copying all of her recipes onto cards for him and put them into a binder as a gift. He didn't cook often, but when he did, he liked to use her recipes as they were ones he pretty much grew up with because he'd spent so much time with her.

Most of us agreed we didn't really have a recipe box or book per se, but most of us had a scribbled recipe on a sheet of paper, cut from a magazine, a card from a family member, or something jotted in the notes on our phones.

Shaw had watched us all in silence before shaking his head. "I'd never really thought about it. My mom had a big box of recipes plus a book she always referred to when she cooked. I have no idea what happened to all of the stuff in our house when she died. I was ten, they took me to an emergency shelter type place the first night and then straight to my new foster family." He'd traced a finger over the recipe card LuLu had written. "Mom was a good cook. I wish I had some of her recipes." He'd laughed, a mixture of bitterness and sadness. "Hell, I wish I had *any* recipes. I've never really eaten a meal if it didn't come from a box or a restaurant."

I'd decided right then and there to do something for Shaw.

The second gift idea came from another comment Shaw had made at our pizza night. Leighton had come home bearing a few big bouquets of flowers.

"Ohhhh, she comes bearing flowers," Ollie had teased as he took some of the blooms from him.

"Can you believe I got these for free? I was walking past the flower shop when the lady was taking them out to put in their composter. I asked why she was wasting them and she said they were too old to sell, but they'd make good fertilizer. I asked her if I could take a few bunches—seriously, she had like a wagon full of them—and she let me. I offered to pay, but she said just tell friends about the shop and we'd count it even. So, y'all be sure to give her business."

"So pretty," Ollie had said. "I think that's where Bash got flowers for the center when he first started there. How many vases do we have?"

Shaw's eyes had gone wide as Ollie and I had gathered four vases from a cabinet.

I'd cocked a brow at Shaw. "You okay?"

He'd nodded. "Yeah, just realizing how unprepared I am for this whole adulting thing. You all have vases. Just on hand. You bring home bouquets to decorate. To decorate an actual home."

As Shaw had watched Leighton, Ollie, and me prepare and arrange the flowers into vases, his face still showing his shock and disbelief, I'd vowed the man would never be without a vase again. And I'd fill it as often as possible if he'd let me.

So, there I stood, repacking the gift bag with a simple recipe book designed to hold up to five hundred recipes, a stack of classic recipe cards, and a pair of flower vases—one for small bouquets and one for larger groupings.

I forced myself to stop questioning the gifts and ran them up to the roof. Checking my phone, I had just enough time to run to the flower shop for a bouquet before Nacho Night started.

Maggie at Cravenwood Flowers was a huge help and didn't make me feel ridiculous when I sputtered around saying I wanted to get a new friend something that meant friendship, family, and love. She seemed to pick up on the fact I wasn't going for full-on romantic love and she smiled reassuringly.

"I've got just the right combination for you. Come around back and you can approve the ones I pick to make a nice bouquet."

That was how I ended up in the back of the flower shop as Maggie showed me different choices to put together a bundle of flowers for Shaw.

"Okay, you mentioned family. The daisy symbolizes family with its innocence and simplicity."

She held up a happy little daisy and I couldn't help but smile as I nodded. "Yes, definitely daisies."

"I really like chrysanthemums and zinnias for friendship. The chrysanthemums show joy and optimism while the zinnias are respect, honor, and remembering those who are no longer with us—maybe not the exact sentiment you're going for—"

"No, that's perfect. He lost his mother. Definitely the zinnias."

Maggie moved to another section of flowers. "Now, we'll steer away from roses if you're not wanting to get too romantic, but showing affection with tulips and carnations is very popular. The tulip often means a perfect love, but we can go with yellow which is a common expression for cheerful thoughts and sunshine."

She added it to the group when I nodded my approval.

"The carnation is definitely a flower of love, but we can stick with the lighter pink which leans more toward gratitude than intimate, romantic love."

"Yes, that's good. I like all of those."

"Perfect, give me a bit of time to put them together with some greenery. Would you like a little card that mentions the meaning of each? Something you can sign your name to? Maybe with your own little message?"

Suddenly, I was terrified of giving Shaw the flowers, but I nodded all the same.

Maggie quickly printed a small piece of cardstock with the meaning of each flower I'd picked and left me to sign a message to it while she built Shaw's bouquet.

Created for you at Cravenwood Flowers.

Your bouquet is filled with blossoms meant to bring a smile to your face.

Daisies for family.

Chrysanthemums for friendship.

Zinnias to remember those we've lost.

Tulips for cheerful thoughts and sunshine.

Carnations for affection.

We hope you love your bouquet.

I STARED at the words for several moments while Maggie hummed to herself as she made magic with the chosen flowers.

Was it too much? Too soon? Were the meanings behind

the flowers over-the-top? Maybe Shaw would read too much into it.

Maybe *I* was reading too much into it.

Swallowing down all the worry, I uncapped the pen and wrote on the card.

We're glad to have you with us as you start this new journey.

To friendship and the family we choose.

Julian

I SIGNED my name before I could talk myself out of it, folded the card and slipped it in the little envelope, and scrawled *Shaw* on the front.

Maggie had the flowers wrapped and tied with a gorgeous ribbon.

I paid and thanked her, promising I'd send business her way.

By the time I made it back to the apartment, I was questioning every single thought and action, but I needed to shower and get ready, so I pushed it all aside.

The main thing I wanted to focus on was a fun night with friends.

Making Shaw feel comfortable and welcome was a nice thing to do.

I refused to let my imagination run wild in the shower, no matter how badly my dick wanted thoughts of Shaw and a slick, soapy hand.

The smell of seasoned meat filled the air when I emerged from the bathroom and I found the crew busily making all the fixings for our rooftop party.

It wasn't our first Nacho Night and it definitely wouldn't

be our last, but I was thrilled knowing Shaw would get to kick back and enjoy his new home with his new friends.

Shaw was quiet as he stared over the rooftop railing.

Like quieter than usual.

Not his normal unsure quiet.

Not his thinking quiet.

This was more a pained, stressed, making decisions he didn't want to be making quiet.

"You know you look at him like he's the only person in the room," Lucas said quietly from his place beside me.

Startled, I jerked my head in his direction. "What? No, I don't. Just worried about him is all."

"Mmhm," Lucas smirked. "Dean, tell him."

"Tell him what?" Ollie piped up.

"That he looks at Shaw with stars in his eyes like he's the only person in the damn room," Dean said, reiterating Lucas's words.

"Oh, well, yeah. Figured that was a given," Ollie agreed. "I mean, anyone with eyes can see that." My little brother threw his arm around me. "But that's between Julian and Shaw, so I'm not getting involved."

Lucas, Dean, and I both snorted and Ollie pretended to be offended.

"What? I don't *have* to stick my nose where it doesn't belong."

"Ohhh, where are we sticking our noses?" Leighton asked, hopping up on Ollie's back and snaking his arms around his best friend's neck.

"We were talking about Julian and Shaw and—" Ollie started.

"And how they are absolutely adorable together and look at each other like they think the other one hung the dang moon? Maybe how they'd like to eat each other alive?" Leighton finished for Ollie. "How they need to kiss and get naked and maybe discuss future little baby Shulians and Jaws?"

I couldn't help but wrinkle my nose. "Little baby *what*?"

"Shulians and Jaws," Leighton said with a grin as if it made complete sense.

"Pretty sure he's shipping the two of you and combining your names for future children," Dean explained with a smile and roll of his eyes.

"I kinda like Shulian," Ollie said. "But I'd draw the line at Jaw. No kid needs to be named Jaw."

"Well, this has been fun, but Jett is here so I'll now be spending the rest of my night in his arms if I have anything to say about it," Leighton said as he sashayed away with a little wave.

"In his arms and on his cock," Lucas teased.

"If wishes come true, you know it, bitch," Leighton agreed over his shoulder.

"I've got goals too," Ollie said as his eyes traveled to where Bash was rolling the aluminum foil out for the nacho bar.

"Well," Lucas said as we watched Ollie beeline toward Bash. "Guess that means you need to go see what's got Shaw looking so melancholy."

I wanted to bring up the fact Lucas and Dean often seemed like more of a couple than some of the actual or potential couples, but I let it drop.

For the time being, and headed toward Shaw.

"You ready to stuff your face with nachos?" I asked as I leaned against the railing next to him.

He turned worried, sad eyes my way. "Not super hungry, but everything smells really good."

I wanted to drag him to the little corner where his gifts and flowers waited, but I got the feeling he'd rather not have any kind of audience right then.

I could wait.

"How's work been?" I asked, hoping to pull him from his funk.

Shaw smiled. "I like it. I think it's the first time I've liked a job and been good at it. The changes I suggested have made everything a lot easier and everyone seems happier—less stressed—so that makes me feel good." He bit his lip like he wanted to say something else, but instead kept up with the small talk. "What about you? Work going ok?"

The last thing I wanted to do was talk about our jobs, but if it meant Shaw was talking and not focusing on whatever had him so down, I'd do it.

We chatted a bit about some of the things I'd been doing around the apartment until the guys called us over.

Even though he'd said he wasn't hungry, Shaw's eyes went wide when we poured two huge bags of chips onto the strip of foil and piled on ground beef, shredded chicken, steak strips, grilled shrimp, and beans. Up and down the strip of foil, there were piles of cheese, tomatoes, onions, lettuce, and globs of sour cream and guacamole, plus bowls of salsa.

"Still not very hungry?" I asked, bumping into him as he took a plate.

"Not starving, but there's no way I can skip all of this." He made himself a small plate from all the fixings and moved to the far corner of the rooftop to eat by himself.

I let him get settled as I made my plate and chatted with the guys.

"How come we didn't get flowers for moving in?" Lucas asked with a shit-eating grin.

Bash snorted but just shook his head.

"Yeah, where's my pretty bouquet and gift bag?" Dean asked, teasing like we'd been friends for ever.

"Shut up, all of you," I grumbled, glancing toward Shaw. "I just want him to feel welcome. The rest of you already had friends here, or made them quickly, he needs to know he's wanted here."

"Then go make him feel welcome," Ollie said, nudging me.

"I hear blow jobs are good for that," Leighton said. "Right, Jett?"

Jett scowled at Leighton, but his cheeks pinked.

I shook my head at my friends and left them to whatever ridiculous conversation they'd come up with.

"Care if I sit?" I asked Shaw, breaking him from whatever deep thinking he was doing.

"No, that's fine. Sorry, I'm kinda out of it and not feeling very much like a party."

"Anything I can do?"

Shaw shook his head, looking miserable. "I don't think so. Maybe? I don't know. I'm just kinda a mess right now."

"That's okay. Just know you've got all of us on your side if you decide to ask for help. We'll do whatever we can."

"I know you would—but you shouldn't have to get involved in my drama. It's mainly my own pride keeping me from sharing anything. Kinda thought I'd left some shit behind, and really don't want to have it catch back up with me."

"Hey, no judgement here. If we don't already have shit in our past, we might have shit waiting on us in our future. None of us will think any different of you, no matter what."

Shaw stared at me for a moment. "The weird part is I want to believe you because I really think you mean it, but you might change your mind." He gestured toward our roommates. "They might not feel the same."

"I get that. Even if it's something that takes us by surprise, or makes us question decisions, we know the you *now*. We like and respect the person you are now. Hell, unless you used to be a serial killer and are still keeping pieces of victims in the freezer or making their skin into furniture, I'm pretty sure there's very little we'd not be able to accept. Even if you were a serial killer, I'm pretty sure most of us would at least try to understand—but we might draw the line at the body parts and skin furniture," I teased, loving the small smile I got from Shaw.

"No murders, promise. Nothing illegal at all. Just things I did to get by—and I don't regret them—I just thought they were part of my past."

"Can I offer something to take your mind off it for a bit?" I asked, putting my plate to the side.

Shaw smiled. "Definitely. I keep trying, but my head keeps going back to it."

I got up motioned for him to follow me.

He eyed me suspiciously when we reached the little corner where I'd hidden the bag and flowers. "So, I'm hoping I wasn't too presumptuous, but I wanted to get you something kinda as a welcome gift." I handed him the bag first.

"You didn't have to get me anything," Shaw said. "You already did too much by taking me shopping and buying me those books." His words were gently accusatory, but he also looked excited to get a gift.

Damn, had no one gotten him gifts after he lost his mom?

My heart tugged and I wanted to make giving him gifts something I did as often as possible.

"Open it. Consider it just a friend helping a friend. It's not anything huge," I said.

He pulled out the recipe book and cards first, his big wide eyes blinking up at me from his perch on the lounge chair.

"So, you said you didn't have any recipes from your mom. We can't really fix that, but I thought this way you could start gathering some. Between the rest of us, I know we've got some recipes worth sharing. We'll fill out cards and you can start your collection."

"That's..." his voice cracked. "That's a very thoughtful gift. Thank you."

I lifted my chin to indicate he should pull out the other items.

"Vases," he said with a huff of laughter.

I shrugged. "You seemed upset you didn't have any—or maybe that you'd never had occasion to have them—so I went with two sizes that should work well with most flowers."

"Thank you. I'm not really used to getting gifts and you're going to spoil me."

"Nah," I said, feeling my cheeks heat. "But there's one more thing."

"Oh my god, Julian, you're too much," Shaw said as I reached for the flowers.

I grimaced as I held them out for him. "Is it? Too much I mean? I wanted to do something nice, but I didn't want to go overboard or make you uncomfortable. I'm sorry if I did."

"No, not at all. I feel bad you got me all this stuff, but I love it all so much. It seems greedy to take it all, but I'm definitely not going to turn it down." He took the flowers and breathed them in deeply. "These are gorgeous. Thank you so much. I'm going to take the small vase to work and put the big one in my room so I can see them all the time." He chuckled. "Well, until they die."

"I'll get you more," I said.

Our eyes met and held.

"Not necessary," he whispered.

"I know. But I think I like buying things for you."

I wanted to kiss him so bad.

Shaw swayed into me, his heat and the scent of his hair product—something orange-ish—teased my senses.

Leighton broke the moment yelling to us about a storm heading in. "Stop flirting and help us get this shit carried downstairs. Soggy nachos are a major buzz kill."

Shaw chuckled as he repacked his gifts and gently placed the flowers in the bag. We made our way toward the food and quickly helped to pack everything back into containers.

The first big drops splattered around us as we ran for the stairs, thunder and lightning chasing us down to the third floor.

"Damn, that was close." Lucas balanced a skillet of meat on top of three bowls. "Who was in charge of weather alerts?"

"I hate rain," Dean complained.

"You always have," Lucas said as we filed into the kitchen to put things together more properly. "Used to bitch and moan about it when we were kids."

"It just makes me feel gross. I don't like it on my skin or my hair, hate the smell of worms that comes with it, and just the general feeling of the air when it rains." Dean put Lucas in a strangle hold. "Sue me. I'm sure I'm not the only person who hates rain."

We fell into a casual conversation as the dishwasher was loaded and food was packed away.

Out of nowhere, Shaw's voice caught my attention.

"No, no, no," he muttered, a panicked whine to his words. "Damn it. No." His eyes were darting from his phone to the guys around the kitchen and living room.

"What?" I asked. "What's wrong? The storm?"

He swallowed, looking as if he was going to puke. "Did any of you get a weird text?"

We all pulled out our phones.

"No, nothing for me," Lucas said.

"Me neither. Why?" Dean asked.

My phone buzzed.

I glanced at the message, to Shaw's devastated face, and back at the message.

BeeJay Love thought he could get away.
   Thought he could hide who he really is.
   But he'll never truly escape.
   Is this the type of man you want living with you?
   He'll never be good for anything but one thing.

A TINY THUMBNAIL video came through under the text.

Without thinking, I clicked the link.

My screen came to life with the title *The Playboy and the Virgin starring Tommy Topper and BeeJay Love*. Then a video came into focus of a younger Shaw sucking a very large dick. Just as my head began to process what I was watching, the scene flipped to Shaw on his hands and knees.

As the man on the screen slid his cock into a visibly distraught Shaw's ass, the air around me filled with the sound of the others' phones getting a text.

"Oh yeah, I got one. Something about BeeJay Love?" Ollie asked.

"Ohhh, kinky. BeeJay Love. I like it." Leighton laughed. "Wait, is this spam? Shaw is your phone catfishing us?"

"Don't click on it," I demanded. "Delete it."

"What's wrong?" Lucas asked, glancing between his phone, me, and Shaw.

"That text sounds pretty threatening," Dean said, concerned eyes landing on Shaw as I wrapped my arm around my trembling friend.

"Delete it. Don't click on the link. Don't reply," I said, my voice confident despite the concern and anger coursing through me.

"Wait," Bash said. "Did everyone get it? We all need to take a screen shot. And one of us needs to save it in case it needs to be used as proof later." I knew Bash had been through some shit with an issue in the past, so he was no doubt the first of us to think about having evidence.

"Fuck," I said, mad at myself for not even thinking of that. "I'll keep it on my phone. The rest of you, take a screen shot if you got the message. Then delete it."

"What's up with that, man? Shaw, you know who sent it? Looks like you got it first, did you know the number? Someone fucking around with you?" Jett asked, his anger evident. He didn't talk a lot, but it was clear he was ready to fight for Shaw.

Tears streamed down Shaw's face. "I'm sorry. I didn't mean for any of you to know about it." He lifted his chin. "I can't make you delete it. I can't ask you not to watch it. But I'll ask anyway. I appreciate the time and energy you guys gave me. I've never really had a group of friends and I've loved every second of living here. I'm really sorry this happened, I'd hoped it was all a bluff."

He rushed toward his room.

"What the fuck?" Ollie asked.

"Screen shot it. Delete the message. And for the love of god, please respect his request." I exited from the video and pocketed my phone.

"Why did it sound like he's leaving?" Leighton asked.

"Because I think that's his plan," I said, moving toward the bedroom.

"He can't leave. He just got here," Ollie said. "I don't know what that text was all about, but it sounded like someone trying to cause problems. We won't watch the video. We don't care about some bullshit text or video. Tell him he can't leave."

I nodded. "I'll do my best." I headed toward Shaw's room.

Tears continued to stain his cheeks as he threw things into his two bags.

"What are you doing?" I asked.

"Leaving."

I gently grabbed his elbow and spun him to face me. "Can't let that happen. We took a vote and we all want you to stay."

One moment, Shaw was staring up at me with tears glistening on his long lashes and the next moment his soft lips were on mine. Heat blossomed between us, my tongue absorbing the sweet flavor of his mouth.

If I'd been worried the spark I thought I'd felt between us was just wishful thinking, the fiery explosion when our lips met discounted that concern.

No kiss had ever lit me on fire the way this one did.

My brain short-circuited, ignoring the tiny voice in the back of my head telling me to stop him. I parted my lips, accepting his seeking tongue as he clung to me, both of us breathing heavily as soft whimpers and moans filled the air.

When Shaw palmed my bulging cock behind my jeans and reached for the button, the voice in my head went into high alert. As much as I loved his lips on mine, as badly as I wanted to feel his hot skin touching me, this wasn't what Shaw needed at the moment.

I gripped his wrist.

"Hey," I said, keeping my words soft and pulling him into my chest when he shuddered with a sob. "As amazing as that was—and I definitely have no problem if we ever want to explore that a bit further—you're hurting and now isn't the time."

"I'm so sorry, I shouldn't have done that." He kept his head buried in my chest.

"Again, don't think I didn't like it, but you wanna tell me what that was all about?" I rubbed my hand up and down his back, wanting to comfort, but feeling extremely out of my league.

"You saw what's on that video, at least a bit of it. That's who I am. That's all I'm good for. It's all you'll see me as now. And that's what they wanted—wanted to punish me for leaving and give me no option but to return." Shaw's eyes never left the floor.

"Hey, I don't want to hear anything like that. First, do not mistake me stopping things as anything close to me not wanting something like that with you. But if you and I ever end up in bed or similar, it will be because you've come to me out of desire, not out of a sense of owing me something. You owe me nothing. You owe none of us anything." I gestured toward the gift bag he'd set right inside the door. "That recipe book? The vases? The flowers? Those were gifts given out of respect and caring friendship. Nothing more, nothing less. No strings attached." I tried to catch his eye, but he wouldn't look away from the floor. "I don't expect anything from you—whether you made one video, a million videos, or none. If we get together, it will be because it's something we both want. Not because you feel bad about your past."

"I did what I had to do back then to survive, but I thought I could start over. Clean slate. I can't. It's catching up with me and I can't put you guys in the path of that. Hell, you couldn't even bring yourself to let them watch it, you don't deserve to have someone with a past like mine living here."

I took his chin in my hand and brought his face close to mine, ignoring the flavor of him still on my tongue and how badly I wanted to explore his mouth for at least the next hour. This wasn't about sex and it wasn't about me.

"I didn't let them watch the video because the only person who should be able to do that is you. If you want them to see it, that's fine. None of us will judge you or think less of you. Whether you did what you did in the past to survive or because you enjoyed it, that's not our business. Whether you left that behind or you plan to continue in that business, it's your choice to make and we have no place to judge. We. Don't. Care." I pressed my forehead against his. "I. Don't. Care." I paused, letting him gather himself. "You're our friend and our roommate. If you choose to tell us about any of your past—if you choose to make any of it part of your present—that's up to you. No one else gets to out your past without your permission. *That's* why I wanted them to delete the text and not watch the video."

Shaw trembled against me and I pulled him close again.

"None of that changes who you are to me, to us," I said.

"How can you be so good about this?" Shaw asked, his words shaky.

"Because that's what friends do. We care about you and we're all here, we're all in this big ol' crazy group together." I waited, enjoying the press of his face on my shoulder. "We can't *make* you stay, but we'd really like it if you did."

"I should tell them what that was all about," Shaw murmured.

"You can if you want, but it's not a requirement. You don't *have* to tell us anything unless you want to."

"I think I want to, but can I tell you first?" Shaw asked, pulling away slightly, his big brown eyes meeting mine.

"Of course. And I'll help you tell them, if you want, when you feel like it's time. We're all here for each other; we don't run when things get tough. You've got us on your side now."

He took a deep, shaky breath.

"Can I take a shower and get ready for bed first?"

"Of course." I let him go, immediately missing the scent of orange cream—I swore his new soap and hair product was already haunting my fantasies. "My room or yours?"

"Let's do mine. I'll probably fall asleep and it'll be easier."

Or you could fall asleep in my bed and I wouldn't care at all.

I nodded. Shaw wasn't ready for sharing a bed or anything more than a friend to listen to him talk. I needed to keep that in mind and let him set the pace.

When he emerged from the bathroom a bit later, I'd already gone to let the guys know a tiny bit of what was going on and assure them I was working to make sure he stayed. As expected, they were all fired up about someone trying to hurt Shaw, and ready to fight if it came down to it.

Shaw settled on his bed.

I took the desk chair despite every cell in my body screaming for me to get into bed with him.

When his eyes lingered on me questioningly, I shrugged. "Figured it would maybe be easier to talk if we had a bit of space. I'll sit wherever you tell me to."

He nodded. "No, that's probably smart. I really am sorry for mauling you earlier."

I chuckled and willed my dick not to get excited all over again. "No harm, no foul. Honestly, don't worry about it—in fact, I'd like to put it out there here and now, I'm down for any and all mauling in the future if it's something you think you'd want, but that's a conversation for another time. Let's get this out in the open. Sometimes just talking about it makes things easier. First though, do you think we need to report the text to the police?"

Shaw's face showed he hadn't given it much thought.

He shook his head. "I'll tell you who I think it is and why. I'm hoping when nothing happens from it, he'll give up. But if something more comes of it, we've got the screen shots and the original on your and my phone, we'll go to them then."

I nodded. "It's your call."

Shaw sighed and launched into his story. "Obviously, you saw the video. I started making adult films when I was eighteen. The first company I was with was run by Benny. He was really nice and knew what he was doing. I didn't *like* making the videos, but I didn't hate it. He got shut down when two of his actors overdosed. He swore he'd reopen, but I didn't have time to wait. I ended up at a company run by this guy named Luka. He was mean. He was making millions, but he wasn't at all caring. I did the videos because I needed the money. I didn't really dislike the guys I shot with, we were all kinda in the same boat for the most part, but I hated every second of it. Luka was an asshole." Shaw took a deep breath. "He played up the virgin angle. Obviously, after my very first video, I wasn't a virgin, but he made me play one in every scene we shot. He got off on making the scenes look non-con or dub-con, always wanted me to look like I didn't want it, like it hurt, that kind of shit."

Shaw was quiet for a moment and I just waited for him to gather his thoughts.

"I left the industry when I was twenty-two. I'd saved up enough money. Luka went ape-shit when he found out I was leaving. Beat me to a pulp. But instead of giving in and going back to him like he wanted, I left anyway." He paused, caught up in the painful memory as I clenched my fists and silently prayed I'd one day get ahold of this Luka. "I found a shit-hole apartment that wouldn't eat into my nest egg. Found a job. And started classes for data entry certification. Pretty quickly, I started dating this guy in the hospital kitchen where we both worked. I decided I really didn't like him and tried to break things off, but he let me know he knew about the videos and threatened to out me to our boss and my instructors. So, I stayed and put up with his shit until I finished classes." He drew his legs up to his chest, wrapping his arms around his knees. "I left him, the job, and the shit apartment at twenty-four and here I am."

I wanted to go to him.

Wanted to avenge this angel-on-earth with any asshole who had ever hurt him.

But I waited.

I wanted Shaw to know I was there and listening.

"I'm sure it's Luka," he said.

"Not Benny or Max?" I asked.

"Benny very likely may be dead by this point, but no, he wasn't cruel. He wanted the best for his boys." Shaw chewed on his bottom lip. "Max had a mean streak, but I didn't lose him money or anything. I'm sure he quickly found someone to take my place and never thought of me again. Luka makes the most sense. I was one of a couple guys bringing in top dollar for him, so when I left, he felt it. It's kinda weird he's taken this long, but if he's been watching me, he knows I'm finally in a position to settle down. I have a place, a job, and friends—he's going to try to ruin that and get me to come back."

"Would you go back?" I asked.

Shaw stared at the window above my head and pursed his lips. "I wouldn't go *back*, but I don't regret it. Even though this has caught up with me, I don't think I'd change much," Shaw mused. "I mean, I'd skip the being beat to shit and just wouldn't have started dating Max, but the decision to make the films was *mine* and they served their purpose. I'm glad I'm not in the position I used to be in, but if I was, I'd probably make the same choice—maybe just go with the more reputable studios knowing what I know now."

He paused again and I could see him trying to organize his thoughts.

"I'm not embarrassed of my body or the sex work." He shook his head, pretty much lost in his thoughts. "I don't judge anyone for sex work. But it's weird how I felt empowered in my choices and the fact those videos allowed me to become more independent and eventually led me here, but they also took so much away from me."

I cocked my head and waited. When he didn't go on, I asked, "What did they take from you?"

Shaw snorted. "Pretty much everything. There's this huge list of all this stuff I've never done—or never got to do on my own terms."

"Like?" I was pretty sure his list would break my heart, but I needed to hear it.

And he needed to share it.

"I'm too tired to get into all of it tonight. Maybe later?"

I was frustrated, but I understood how the events of the day were very likely catching up to Shaw and exhausting him. "Sure thing. But I need you to know nothing you've told me tonight is a reason for you to leave. We're here for you. I'm here in whatever capacity you need."

Shaw smiled sleepily. "Thank you for making this easier."

I stood to leave, making my way to the door.

"Holding hands with a guy," Shaw mumbled sleepily as he curled under his blanket. "There's so much—too damn much got taken from me—but just simply holding hands with a guy is something I've never done."

I thought he was going to say more, but he drifted to sleep the moment his head hit the pillow.

If he'd have me, I'd hold hands with him from here to eternity.

I closed his door and headed to my room.

Too damn much got taken from me.

That kid had lost so much and knowing there was more that had been taken from him had my heart twisting in my chest.

I glanced at the text on my phone.

Was it from Luka?

Would the man truly try to ruin the blossoming life Shaw was attempting to start?

The video icon tempted me from the screen.

I refused to click on it.

Refused to watch the video.

Hell, I'd maybe never watch porn again since I knew there was a chance I'd see Shaw. It wasn't like I'd search him out, but if he was with two fairly decent-sized production companies, there was a definite probability I'd see one of his scenes.

Not that I didn't want to imagine him naked and writhing under me.

But watching those films felt like a blatant intrusion of his privacy.

Yeah, he'd known they'd be available for all to see when he made them.

But me watching them, knowing him, felt wrong on many levels.

Instead of thinking about the video I'd seen, I climbed into the shower and imagined where that kiss might have led if it had been the right time.

With the image of Shaw on his knees for me dancing through my head, I jerked myself off. Completely spent, I leaned against the cool tile.

Shaw had been through so much.

And he had more to tell me.

My only option was to be there as a friend and let him make the move if he wanted us to be more.

If he didn't, then I predicted a lot more jerking off in the shower in my future.

FIVE

Shaw
_____

OVER THE NEXT COUPLE WEEKS, I found time to talk with most of my roommates.

No one seemed to have a problem with my past, although all of them seemed ready to fight Luka if it came down to it.

Leighton and Ollie were the most supportive—aside from Julian who had become my knight in shining armor even though I didn't *need* saving, but it was nice to have a protector all the same.

"Hey, bae," Leighton said from the doorway of our shared bathroom.

"Christ, Leigh," I exclaimed, jumping about a foot in the air and nearly wiping out in the shower. "Knock?"

"Sorry," he said, not sounding at all sorry. "First, you need to hide your new scents before I steal them. Second, where did you get them? They're fabulous."

I'd splurged with one of my first paychecks from the health center and gotten a collection of really nice soap, shampoo, lotion, and hair product in an orange cream scent. It maybe wasn't a typical masculine scent, but I remembered my mom smelling of oranges and the scent was comforting.

"I ordered it online. You can't have it. Can't I shower in peace?" I didn't really mind having Leighton in the bathroom while I showered, but he was fun to tease.

"Can't have what? Damn, you smell good," Ollie said, popping in on the impromptu bathroom party.

"Right? I want to share his soap, but he says I can't," Leighton said.

"Oh my god, both of you, can you get out? How am I supposed to get ready to go meet LuLu if you're both pervin' on me in the shower?" I loved them like the brothers I never had and knew without a doubt the three of us weren't at all into each other, but I liked to give them a rough time.

It was somewhat overwhelming to me just how quickly I'd grown to love and trust the new men in my life.

"Fine, but hurry up, we need to leave soon," Ollie said.

I knew he was excited to introduce us to Bash's aunt, LuLu—who Ollie swore loved him more than Bash and wanted to adopt him.

They left and I finished up, drying off and styling my hair —my head never far from Julian and what a big part of my heart he'd stolen.

I wanted more with him.

And he'd indicated he wanted the same.

But I needed to make sure he knew *all* of my past before I could jump into anything with him. Maybe it was selfish, but I wanted him to know all the things I'd lost my say in so he'd understand my wants and desires—understand where I was coming from and what I needed to make a relationship successful.

Not that I really had any idea how to make a relationship successful.

But I knew what did *not* work—Max had shown me that. Not that I'd ever felt an iota of what I felt for Julian with Max.

I knew what my heart longed for.

Julian.

It was as simple as that.

Some would argue I couldn't trust my heart if it fell for the very first man who showed me any sort of kindness.

I would argue my heart knew exactly what it wanted after being around the worst of the worst most of my life. The fact Julian came along when he did was fate and I wasn't going to question it or try to escape it.

I was surrounded by gorgeous, wonderful men in my home. I was slowly getting to know folks around Cravenwood Block. There were amazing people at my work.

But my heart had set its sights on Julian.

No one else would do.

But he deserved to know every single part of me before getting too involved.

Maybe it was too much.

Maybe he wouldn't have the energy or resolve to put up with someone who needed the chance to make up for what I'd missed in the past.

If that was the case, my heart would need to find a new reason to beat.

I scoffed at myself in the mirror, the luscious scent of orange cream clinging to the air. I realized moving away from the horrors of my past only to find my heart beating for one man in particular was likely not the healthiest thing I could be doing.

And I wasn't fool enough to believe I'd only be complete with Julian by my side.

But I'd missed out on a lot of my teen angst years—didn't have time for melodrama when I was too busy surviving actual drama—so allowing my emotions the chance to play and be dramatic wouldn't hurt anything.

As an adult of fairly sound mind and realistic

expectations, I knew if Julian didn't want a relationship with me—or couldn't deal with the somewhat extra care and energy I might require—I'd continue to be his friend and eventually, maybe, move on to a healthy relationship down the road.

As a man not far removed from my teen years, in which I lost out on a lot of the usual teen theatrics and emotional tension related to very teenage type things, I reserved the right to claim—at least in my own head—my heart would beat for only one. And if that *one* didn't reciprocate, I'd vow to live the rest of my life in mourning over what could have been.

I rolled my eyes at myself, smirking at how ridiculous I was being.

Heading into my room to get dressed, I glanced again at the flowers Julian had given me. They were so absolutely perfect and I imagined the serious concentration on his face as he wrote the message and signed his name.

He likely questioned if the meanings of the flowers were too much.

If his little note was overboard.

If he was crossing a line.

But I loved every single bloom, leaf, meaning, and letter of the entire message he'd given to me.

Friendship, affection, family—the way he openly allowed me to celebrate and remember my mom—that was what I had with Julian.

Yes, I wanted more.

But I didn't see a need to rush.

"I think he's the real-deal, Mom," I whispered to my empty room.

Was I being presumptuous and ridiculous to think a man eleven years older than me would want to dive into a relationship with someone who brought *a lot* of baggage to the table?

Maybe.

But there was no mistaking the fire in that kiss.

Perhaps it had been ill-timed—I did regret letting my emotions overtake the situation and appreciated Julian putting a stop to it until I was in a better place—but he'd wanted me just as much as I wanted him.

Would he be willing to give me what I needed if we revisited the topic of an intimate relationship?

"I think I could love him," I murmured to the ghost of my mother. "I know I can take care of myself—I've proven that—but having him on my side, supporting me and loving me, if he'll have me, sounds like my fairytale dream come true."

Of course, he'll have you I heard my mom say. Perhaps I'd exaggerated her personality over the years, but I knew she was my biggest fan, staunchest supporter, and she loved my heart more than anyone. *You're Shaw Elliot Fenton and any man would be lucky to have you. Let him love you and don't be afraid to show him who you are and love him in return.*

Maybe I misused my memories of my mom to pump myself up—did I really remember her that well after fourteen years?—but I needed the encouragement and peace her memory brought me.

I couldn't remember her voice or laughter anymore, although her smile and scent hadn't yet vanished, but I'd never forget her fierce protection and love for me.

And I saw the same in Julian.

"You ready yet, sweet cheeks?" Leighton asked from the doorway.

"Yep, let's go." I shoved my phone in my pocket and followed Leighton to the front door where Ollie was waiting. "Is Bash going with us?"

"No, he's working on something at the center. Plus, LuLu

asked for just me and my friends to come. I think today is the day she'll let me know she loves me more than Bash." Ollie grinned, ever the jokester.

"Haven't you only been around her a couple times?" I asked.

"She loved me from the moment she met me," Ollie said, pretending to swoon.

We headed toward the retirement home where Ollie's dad, Roger, worked and Bash's aunt, LuLu, lived.

"You seem all up in your head," Leighton said, bumping his hip against mine.

I pulled myself from the clouds. "Sorry, just thinking." I shrugged. "I'm not used to having people around I can trust and talk to. It's usually just me and my books. I've gotten really good at escaping into fictional worlds—having you guys is new."

"Don't ever forget we're here." Ollie threw an arm around me. "I know this is all new and you have every right to move into it slowly, take some time to get used to all of us, but we're here. We support you." He jostled me. "I'm even all for you and my brother getting it on if it comes to that."

"I second that notion," Leighton said with a sunshiney smile. "You and Julian are absolutely adorable together. I get you've been smart taking your time and getting to know him, but I swear to you, he's the best."

I couldn't help the heat flushing my cheeks as they talked about Julian and me. "Thanks. It's weird to not regret my past, but still not want it splashed all over my present. I really appreciate the whole group being so accepting."

"Look, sex work is valid. However you chose to survive back then—and even if you want to continue it now—we accept you," Ollie said. "We just want you safe and content—it's the same we want for all of us."

"Yep," Leighton agreed. "You maybe didn't come here

looking for your forever family, but that's what you've found. Sorry, baby doll, you're stuck with us."

I'd found my family.

My throat thickened with emotion.

Found family.

He was right.

That's what these men were to me.

From the moment my mom died, I'd been on a desperate, painful, endless journey to find love, acceptance, stability, and belonging.

I'd struck out time and time again.

Until I found myself on Cravenwood Block and wrapped up in the welcoming arms of seven of the most amazing men I'd ever met.

I croaked out an acknowledgement of some sort, but I think the guys understood I was a bit choked up.

"Okay, so I maybe overshared a bit with LuLu about your past," Ollie started as we walked through the doors. "Sorry about that, I tend to have that habit."

"You told Bash's aunt about my past in gay porn?" I asked as we stopped in front of a door labeled 5B.

Ollie grimaced. "Yes, and I realize that wasn't really my place, but she's got a past herself and she's very open and understanding. You're going to love her and she might even have some great advice."

"It's all good," Leighton said. "She's family."

A woman I guessed to be about seventy-ish opened the door with a broad smile, her short, spiky gray hair looking freshly styled. "Come in, come in. I've been looking so forward to meeting Ollie's friends."

She led us to her small living room and offered butterfly pea flower tea and shortbread cookies.

"I don't bake much unless I'm making my special brownies, but it's amazing what you can get delivered these days," she said, gesturing for us to sit and help ourselves. "Now, let me guess. The sunshiney blond has to be Leighton. And this dark-eyed beauty must be Julian's angel-on-earth, Shaw."

I nearly choked on my tea.

"Awww," Ollie crooned. "Did Dad tell you that's what Julian called him? That's so damn sweet."

"Roger says Julian is pretty much smitten," LuLu said. "But I maybe shouldn't reveal all Julian's secrets." She took a bite of cookie and studied me. "So, Shaw, I hear you've had a time of it."

My cheeks flamed.

"Now, don't be all embarrassed, Ollie didn't tell me to cause problems. But I want you to know, I have a bit of a past myself."

I cocked a brow and took another cookie as Ollie and Leighton appeared to get comfy for story time.

"I was a teen during the summer of love. I wasn't thinking about future jobs, I only wanted to feel good, love everyone, and let my voice be heard." LuLu had a far-off gleam in her eyes. "I spent many a day marching in protests and burning bras—now, let me tell you, the whole *burning* bras is pretty much a myth, but I *will* say a lot of females happily shed their bras in support of rights. Now, I maybe found myself in the heat of summer, happily high on some good stuff, waving my bra around with no shirt on in the middle of a protest march. And that image was possibly caught on film. Nothing much came of it as I was just an unknown protestor at an event outside of my hometown.

"However, about five years later, I started working at a place where I hoped to eventually be part of the dieticians on staff. But one of my male colleagues got...I believe you kids call it butt-hurt these days...because I was picked for a project he'd put his name in for. Well, the man was determined to see me ousted. He must have spent months looking for *something* to dig up and hold against me. After what I'm guessing was hours and hours on the microfiche machine—I'm sure you boys don't even know what that is— he found the picture and threatened to show it to my boss unless I took myself off the project."

Ollie leaned in, just as into the story as I was. "What did you do?"

"I yanked the photograph from him and marched into my boss's office. Showed it to him, told him it was from a time in my life I was actually quite fond of because I was standing up for what was right, told him I wasn't in the least bit ashamed of myself or my body, and threw that weasly little asshole right under the bus by exposing his attempt to blackmail me." LuLu's face told the story of how proud she was of that moment in her life as she brushed crumbs from her hands. "My colleague was fired and I was promoted. I didn't end up staying there for long, but I always appreciated my boss doing the right thing."

She turned to me.

"So, I know a little bit about what you're going through. Nothing you've done in your past is worth being ashamed of. You're a survivor, you did what was best for you, and sex work is valid work. No shame." She sipped her tea. "If I were you, I'd do exactly what you're doing right now. Call their bluff. Hold onto the text and video as evidence. Keep on keepin' on." She winked with a wicked smile. "And maybe make some new videos with a certain apartment manager for your future foreplay and viewing pleasure."

"Oh my god," Ollie whispered as I nearly choked to death on my cookie. "I love you so much."

The rest of the visit was easy and fun, even though I couldn't get the idea of watching a video of Julian and me out of my head.

When we finally said goodbye, LuLu made us promise to visit often and I knew we would.

"If you make a video with Julian, can you blur out your faces so I can watch?" Leighton asked.

"God, no," Ollie said. "I can't watch my brother having sex." He waggled his brows at me. "But I think the video idea has merit. Make a video with someone you actually like and use it to replace the negative aspects of the past? Good call, LuLu, good call."

I wasn't sure about the video idea, only because I didn't know where things with Julian and me were going, but LuLu's story had given me hope. I felt better about myself and knowing I'd done nothing wrong.

It wasn't as if I hadn't been telling myself the same thing, but hearing it from friends and an older, more experienced person just made it better.

Luka could kiss my ass.

"So sweet that Julian called you his angel-on-earth." Leighton sighed as we walked. "He's definitely smitten with you."

I couldn't help the fluttering in my belly and the smile tugging at my lips.

Did Julian really think of me that way?

Maybe things between us could go somewhere after all.

————

ABOUT A WEEK LATER, we discovered Bash and Ollie shared a birthday—which was actually really cool when I thought about it. Like a happy little twist of fate to seal whatever will-they-won't-they thing the two of them had going on.

In a whirlwind of comments and questions, it was determined all eight of us were available for a road trip to

Wild Ride, an amusement park not too terribly far away, to celebrate Bash's and Ollie's birthday.

When I'd first heard the plans, my heart had sank knowing Dean and I would likely have to work, but then I'd realized it was our weekend off. I didn't want to assume I'd be invited, but it appeared it was just a given.

For a brief moment, Bash seemed to balk and try to get out of going, which led to Leighton saying he *had* to go or there would be an odd number. I didn't want to, but I offered to stay home as well, so there'd be an even number if Bash didn't go.

"No way, you're going," Julian had said and shot a glare toward Bash. "The fact all eight of us can go so easily means we should definitely take advantage of it. We could all use a weekend away."

Not going to lie, Julian insisting I went on the trip with them had my heart fluttering and a perma smile teasing my lips.

Lucas got the room, Dean purchased the tickets and we just paid him for them, and Julian rented the van because he was able to get a really good discount.

Me? I just soaked up the feeling of being wanted and included. I had good memories of going to an amusement park with my mom before she died, but I'd been too short to ride the really big rides, so the idea of a full day of roller coasters with friends sounded great.

The evening of the trip, eight of us piled into a rented 12-passenger van. Julian punched in the address to Wild Ride and we headed off. The plan was to stop for a quick dinner, arrive at our hotel by ten o'clock, get a decent night's sleep, and hit the park when they opened on Saturday morning. We'd stay until closing, sleep at the hotel, and drive back Sunday morning.

Our stop for dinner turned out to be a lot of fun. It was

amazing to me how much easier and more enjoyable it was to have actual friends and no one trying to control you in order to make a buck.

I sometimes wondered about some of the guys who were in the industry with me. The guy who was just using the films to save money for acting classes. The guy who said he was just doing it to prove to his highly religious family he could do it and God wouldn't strike him dead on the spot. The guy who started in the industry as a reporter, but ended up staying because the money was so good—I thought he still wrote stories for different publications under an alias.

There were the guys who just really liked the scene and didn't even think about leaving.

There were definitely more guys like me who didn't feel bad about the videos and knew the money was the only thing keeping us from the gutter, but didn't love the way all aspects of sexual intimacy had been taken away from us—or at least that's the way it seemed for me.

I knew there were at least three of us who felt the same when Benny's company shut down and we found ourselves at Luka's. I wouldn't have called us *friends*, but we were kinda birds of a feather.

We weren't the loud party-goers.

We weren't the ones bragging online about scenes we were doing.

Luka used to get pissed because I didn't post like twenty times a day trying to get interest in my next video.

Thing was, and he admitted it in a drunken rage once, I didn't have to do much promo. People loved the whole innocent virgin's first time angle and they ate up anything and everything I was in. If my scene partner talked it up in teaser posts, all the better, but I could make a video, not say a word, and hit record numbers the day it landed on the site.

Some of the guys didn't like that.

Some of them loved it and wanted to be in scenes with me all the time.

I figured a lot of the guys who were still with Luka were glad I was gone, but I had a feeling quite a few missed riding on my coat tails.

And I knew the money I lost for Luka was what fueled him into trying to blackmail me. I hated he'd dragged my friends into the mess, but I wasn't going to give in to him. I wasn't going back, not when I had so much ahead of me.

"Hey, you good?" Leighton asked, jumping on my back as we headed out of the restaurant toward the van.

"Yeah," I said, laughing and pulling my head from the downer thoughts. "I've never been on a road trip before, this is fun."

Leighton kissed my cheek. "Stick with us, sugar, we're all kinds of fun."

I smiled as he launched himself from my back and ran to catch up with Jett. Those two were as different as night and day, but they'd found something with each other that seemed really good. As far as I could tell, for the time being, they were taking things between them as a friends-with-benefits situation, but I had a feeling it was more than that if either of them would be honest with themselves.

Once we were back on the road, Ollie took song suggestions from his cuddly little place next to Bash—who looked to be *trying* to hate his life, but I really didn't think he was too upset to have Ollie nestled against him—while the rest of the crew laughed and sang. I knew it was only because everyone else had kinda coupled-up, but I loved the fact I was sitting up front with Julian.

A while later, the GPS directed Julian to take a right and soon we were pulling up to an apartment complex type location. "I thought we got a hotel," Julian said.

"No, I said I'd call about a room," Lucas said. "I went the

AirBnB route. The one I got has two bathrooms and sleeps eight. We're really only here to sleep, right? Figured we didn't need anything fancy."

No one could really argue with the logic, and the building looked to be clean and well-kept in a decent part of town.

"It's close to the park, too. We'll be able to head out early, grab breakfast, and be in line before the gates open," Dean added. I got the feeling at least a few of my new friends had a lot of experience with amusement parks.

We unloaded the van as Lucas fiddled with the key code on the door.

Before long, the eight of us were standing in the middle of a creatively renovated apartment. The owners had obviously taken advantage of the AirBnB mindset and their close proximity to the amusement park when they remodeled the apartment.

"From the listing, it seems like they've got other units on property that sleep only two to four people, and I thought about getting two of those," Lucas explained. "But this one could fit us all and it was dirt cheap due to a last-minute cancellation."

The lodging had clearly once been two separate studio apartments, but the shared wall had been cut out and replaced with an interesting archway between the two. Four king-sized beds took up most of the space in both halves of the apartment, with only a desk, dresser, bedside table, and two floor lamps squeezed in on each side of the shared arch.

I couldn't help but smile as Leighton and Jett threw their bags on one of the beds and made their way to one of the bathrooms to *save water* in a shared shower. Then, my attention turned to Lucas tackling Dean onto one of the beds.

"Do you think they'll ever admit it?" I quietly asked Julian.

"Eventually, yeah," Julian said. "One of them is going to

finally be hit smack dab in the face with the realization—I just hope it's before either of them has settled down."

Ollie snorted. "There's no way they're settling unless it's with each other. They are attached at the hip—connected heart-to-heart with an invisible tether. Yeah, I think they'll eventually see what's right in front of them."

As I glanced around the rooms at the bed Jett and Leighton had claimed, the bed Lucas and Dean were wrestling on, and the two remaining beds, I realized there was a very real possibility Julian and I might be expected to share a bed.

Or maybe I'd share with Bash?

It wasn't that I didn't like the guy, but I wasn't sure I was comfortable sleeping with him. Plus, I figured Ollie would kill me if I took his chance to get up close and personal with his guy.

"Um, I can sleep on the floor…" I suggested.

"No one is sleeping on the floor," Julian said.

A lot of unspoken messages were shared between Ollie, Julian, and Bash while I waited to see how everything would play out.

Finally, Bash tossed his bag onto the bed where Ollie had stretched out.

So, I guessed I was sleeping with Julian.

Cool.

Cool, everything was totally cool.

It was just a bed.

I was cool.

It was cool.

Everything was cool.

Everyone eventually got through showers and settling into bed for an early morning wakeup.

The bed I was sharing with Julian was big, and we'd been closer in my bed at home when he came in for my nightmares, but my heart still kicked up a notch at the idea of sleeping with him.

I'd never slept with another person.

I had my own bed when I was with my mom.

I had my own bed when I was with my first foster family.

After that, I usually got a crappy bed or a couch. Sometimes the floor.

Max never wanted me to sleep over, not that I ever wanted to anyway. Sex with him had always left me feeling degraded, empty, and more alone than ever before.

So, I had no clue if I was a bed hog or anything.

The room was dark, only the dim light filtering in through the curtains producing shadows. The rest of the group was either asleep, getting comfortable, or whispering softly, so I didn't think anyone would mind Julian and me having a quiet conversation.

Pulling on my courage and brushing off my rusty flirting skills—and by rusty, I meant pretty much non-existent—I turned to my side to face Julian. "Sorry ahead of time if I'm a bed hog or steal your covers."

Julian chuckled and turned toward me. "It's all good. I'm sure there are a lot of worse things that could happen." He propped his head on his elbow. "Never held hands with a guy. Tell me something else you've never done."

There was *a lot* on that list, but I figured in keeping with the fun of the weekend, I'd stick to the lighter ones.

"Well, like I told Leighton earlier, I've never been on a road trip like this. So, I can check that one off the list."

"What else?" Julian asked, his warm, clean scent teasing me. I swore he'd somehow moved closer.

"I've never been on an actual date. You know, guy comes to the door. Brings flowers, takes me to dinner and a movie. The flowers you got me were the only ones I've ever gotten."

"I'm glad I got them then," Julian answered softly. "What else?"

"Never had a pet on my own. Mom and I had a cat when I was little, but I never got to have a pet after she died." I chuckled. "I loved that damn cat."

"The apartment allows pets with a deposit," Julian said. "If you wanted to get one."

"Think the guys would mind?"

"Nah, I'm sure they'd actually love having a cat around."

We were quiet for a few moments.

"There are other things, but it's more than I want to talk about on a fun weekend," I said.

"Thank you for sharing with me."

I continued to face Julian despite the conversation coming to a natural end. I should have rolled to my back and gone to sleep. Instead, I stayed on my side, my left arm propped under my head and my right arm tucked under my pillow, only my pinky peeking out.

Julian, in a position mirroring me, shifted his left hand on the mattress.

Our pinkies brushed together and all the air rushed from my lungs.

My blood ran hot.

The butterflies in my stomach took flight.

And instead of freezing like I would have thought, I moved my little finger, purposely brushing against Julian's again.

Without a single word, his eyes never leaving mine in the dimly lit room, Julian shifted his hand so he could curl his fingers around mine.

The heat of our skin, the memories of the kiss we'd shared and what I'd offered to do before Julian stopped me, and the ever-present thrum of attraction between us had me wanting to lean in and kiss him.

Curl into him.

Let him hold me as I slept.

Wake up to his sleepy kisses.

But his gentle warmth, his hand holding mine, sent sparks through my blood.

It was enough.

For the time being, Julian holding my hand was all I needed.

"Thought I could help you check off another item on your list," Julian said gruffly.

"Is that the only reason?" I asked, not wanting to admit how disappointed I'd be if he'd only taken my hand to mark an item off my list.

"Not even close," Julian whispered, squeezing my hand and running his thumb over the back of my knuckles.

I couldn't help the smile as I gave his hand a little squeeze of my own and snuggled into the pillow to sleep.

Several moments later, I woke myself when I rolled to my back and pulled my hand from Julian's grip. Even in my sleepy state, the butterflies in my stomach shifted into overdrive when Julian rolled to his back as well, but reached his right hand out to capture my left.

The gentle clasp of his hand against mine was absolutely everything.

I was wanted.

I was safe.

I belonged.

With this group of people, and more specifically, if the warm fingers curled around mine were any indication, with a man who had quickly become a friend, a protector, and hopefully more.

And I wouldn't have had it any other way.

I fell asleep as content and hopeful as I'd ever been.

The next morning, the guys gave Bash shit for being all

cuddled up with Ollie, but Julian broke the possible awkwardness by asking me to walk with him to grab coffee.

When we got back, laden down with a chai latte for Leighton, some sort of herbal tea for Ollie because they didn't have his favorite, hot chocolate for me, and coffee for the rest of the guys, everyone was ready.

They doctored up their coffees as needed, we grabbed backpacks, and piled into the van. The plan was to grab breakfast at the diner we'd passed on the way in and be in line for the park before it opened.

How did diner food taste so delicious? I figured it was because the eight of us squeezed into a circular corner booth and laughed throughout our meal.

Once we finished eating and found a spot to park, we started the process of packing the backpacks with essentials and slathering on sunscreen. Leighton, Ollie, and Lucas were the most likely to burn. Jett had a lot of ink to protect so he applied the SPF liberally as well.

The day had dawned absolutely gorgeous.

If we'd spent months planning the perfect weekend, it wouldn't have turned out as great as this last-minute trip.

We pretty much stayed together the whole day, partnered up in our natural pairs.

Jett and Leighton.

Lucas and Dean.

Ollie and Bash.

And lucky me, Julian and Shaw.

The roller coasters were amazing.

The first one we went on was called Riptide and I loved every single second of it. I think we ended up riding it five times that day.

Later, when Ollie, Leighton, and I went to one of the shops, I couldn't help the giggle bursting from me when I bought a shirt with the words *I Lost My Virginity on Riptide and*

All I Got Was This Lousy T-Shirt, but the words *Roller Coaster* were slightly hidden between *My* and *Virginity* written on a screen print of the Riptide track.

It wasn't something I'd be wearing to work or out in public, but it was a perfect memento of our weekend.

The pink of Julian's cheeks and the flare of his nostrils when he saw what my new shirt later said was well worth the ridiculous thirty-five dollars. Maybe I'd rip the sleeves off and wear just the shirt if I ever got Julian to help me with the list of things I wanted to do now that I was making my own decisions about intimate relationships.

By the time we dragged ourselves into the rented apartment after spending the entire day at the park, we were all exhausted. Showers were short and sweet, and everyone basically collapsed into bed.

"You smell good," Julian mumbled sleepily as I cuddled under the comforter. "Oranges. Always like oranges."

My heart clenched in my chest at the thought Julian knew what I smelled like.

When his hand reached for mine, I smiled into the dark.

But when he rolled to face me, moving our clasped hands to my chest, and pressing his leg against mine, I nearly forgot to breathe.

"You have fun?" he asked in gruff whisper.

"Yeah, it was great."

"Good," he said, pressing a kiss to my shoulder. "'Night."

The butterflies were back and they were happier than ever.

SIX

Julian

WHEN WE GOT HOME from our road trip to Wild Ride, everyone kinda dispersed to do their own thing.

Shaw had cuddled up in a chair with a book and spent hours immersed in his fictional world. I had a feeling he needed a slight break from all the people-ing before he headed back to work.

The whole crew fell back into our routine—which was mostly no routine.

Lucas often worked days, but he'd sometimes take late shifts if Dean was working late. Those two either had no clue how entwined their lives were or they just didn't care. I really wasn't sure how they'd survive if they weren't attached at the hip.

Shaw mostly worked days, but occasionally had a late shift—I appreciated that Dean usually finagled the schedule so Shaw's late nights matched Dean's. Cravenwood Block was about as safe as you could get, but I didn't like the idea of Shaw walking home after a late shift. Dean being with him meant I didn't have to come up with some excuse to walk him home.

Ollie and Bash usually only worked days, but often worked late or went in to finish things up on the weekends. They had what many would refer to as a school-day schedule, but since they were open over school breaks as well, they worked pretty much year-round with the exception of Thanksgiving week, two weeks at Christmas, and shortened hours over the summer.

My job was pretty much twenty-four-seven, but Chloe was a godsend and my maintenance crew were worth their weight in gold. We were all pretty much on-call all the time, but we balanced who took each call so no one was constantly swamped—unless it ended up being one of those weeks where every single thing seemed to break all at once.

Leighton and Jett probably had the least set schedules, but they somehow managed to mostly match their work hours up—or at least spend chunks of time together between shifts. Jett had started waking up with Leighton when our barista friend had an early shift, and Leighton often found himself at the tattoo shop after his late shifts. In between, the two could almost always be found spending their breaks with each other.

With everyone out or at work, I found myself smack dab in the middle of an odd night where I ended up being home by myself when a knock sounded softly at my bedroom door.

After warding off a heart attack because I'd thought I was alone in the apartment after my shower, I cracked the door open to find my very own angel-on-earth standing there with a sheepish smile.

"Hey, I thought you were at work?" I said, pulling the door open wide.

"I was, but there was some scheduling glitch and they sent me home since the other person on shift had fewer hours than me this week."

"Ollie and Bash went out on a date and everyone else is at work," I said, feeling dumb for stating the obvious.

Shaw bit his lip. "Would you want to order some food and maybe watch a movie?"

Would I want to spend an evening with Shaw?

Was this a trick question?

"Sure, sounds good. You wanna shower and I'll order something?"

Shaw nodded. "Meet you in the living room? Or in here?"

It would have likely been smarter to stay in the living room, however, my libido—which wasn't usually super ramped up, had decided to kick into gear around Shaw—voted for the privacy of my bedroom.

"Just come on in here. You want pizza, Chinese, or subs?"

"That deli sounds good. Can you get me the same as what we ordered last time?" He shifted his work bag on his shoulder and I couldn't help but notice how hot he looked in his scrubs.

I pulled up the order app on my phone and scrolled through. "Turkey, cheese, avocado, bacon, and barbeque chips?"

"Yes, please. I can send you the money."

"Nah, don't sweat it, I've got a free sandwich on here anyway."

Shaw smiled and started to walk away, but he turned back around. "Um, maybe after the movie, we can…talk?"

I wasn't sure what he wanted to talk about, but I would have agreed to just about anything if it meant spending time with him.

Whether I thought it was a good idea or not, Shaw had quickly—and oh, so easily—become a huge and highly enjoyable part of my life.

Thirty-minutes later, my citrus-scented angel and I had a bedroom picnic while we tried to decide on a movie to watch.

By the time I gathered up the trash and tossed it in the kitchen garbage can, we were no closer to actually picking a title than before.

"Are you set on a movie?" Shaw asked.

"Nah, not really. What did you want to talk about?" I stretched out on my side to face him, trying to convince myself being in bed with him could remain completely platonic.

And it *could*.

I'd never force anything sexual if Shaw wasn't on board. That had never been my M.O. and never would be.

But trying to tell myself I was feeling *only* platonically toward Shaw was an absolute waste of time.

I wanted more with him.

So much more.

But I knew he needed to set the pace and make the calls.

"Well, we'd been talking about things I'd never done. Thought I'd tell you a bit more about that."

"I'm always ready to listen to whatever you want to tell me." I wanted to take his hand—something in him, or between us, called to me like never before—but I held back, thinking it would maybe be easier for Shaw if I left that up to him.

"Well, I started in the adult film industry when I was eighteen. There was all kinds of underage drinking, but I skipped out on all drinking from the very beginning because I saw some guys get in a lot of trouble—both from being involved in providing the alcohol, getting way too sloshed, and some fuckers taking advantage." Shaw sat on the bed, facing me, his bare arms teasing me from the torn-off sleeves of his Riptide shirt, bare legs in shorts tucked under him. "So, getting drunk is something I've never done. I know the hangover would likely suck, but I'd like to do it at least once.

I've just never felt safe enough to get drunk around the people I used to work or hang out with."

My heart hurt for the kid. Not because he'd never been drunk, but because he'd never been in a situation where he'd felt safe enough to let loose like that.

"We could always have a party with just the eight of us. I bet Lucas would mix you some drinks to try."

His face brightened. "Seriously?"

"Sure. I mean, there's nothing illegal about it for any of us. We'd keep you safe." I poked his leg. "I'd even help you through the hangover."

"Awww, that's so sweet. Let's do it."

"Deal. We'll get something set up." Instead of spreading my hand out on the warm skin of his leg, I moved my fingers back to the mattress between us. "What else?"

"Well, I never got to go to a prom." Shaw scrunched up his nose. "I was never at one school long enough to really build a group of friends and I definitely wasn't asking a guy to the prom when I was already pretty much an outcast. I always told myself it was just a dance and was likely overrated, but sometimes I just wish I could have gone."

God damn, the kid was killing me.

"Would it help if I told you I went to one prom and didn't go to my senior one because it really, truly *is* overrated?" I asked.

Shaw smiled. "Maybe a little." He picked at a thread on the comforter. "So, the cat, the date, drinking, prom, those are all pretty simple things. I don't know why I feel so comfortable with you, but if you want to hear the rest, I'll tell you."

"You can tell me anything you want." I got the feeling he hadn't had a confidant of any type since his mom. Whether I was just a listening ear or something more, I wanted to be there for him.

"I don't look at virginity as something sacred, but it pisses me off I didn't get to decide who I gave mine to. Didn't get to decide when and where it happened. I was nervous as hell, but they all just laughed it up and said it made for *real* emotion on-screen."

Shaw paused as if lost in the memory and I fought to control my anger. I wasn't one for violence, but I once again found myself wanting to harm the people who had treated my angel so badly.

"He fucked me for the first time over a dresser for a scene —I don't even remember his real name, just what he was known as in the industry. And then I filmed at least five more virgin scenes that week, each with a different guy. Turned out, the first guy was actually the most patient and made things as easy as possible for me. The rest of them weren't *bad*, but everything was just so detached.

"I've always said I don't regret the films—and that's the honest truth—I just wish the chance to make decisions hadn't been taken from me." He paused and pulled his legs to his chest, wrapping his arms around his knees. "I've never had the chance to initiate sex—never had the chance to just have sex because it was what we both wanted instead of what was expected because I was being paid."

Scowling, I brushed my knuckles over his bare feet. "What about the boyfriend? Max?"

Shaw laughed bitterly. "Well, he wasn't *paying* me, but letting him fuck me was definitely expected. He used the films against me and threatened to tell my school and work if I didn't do what he wanted.

"That's another thing. I've never really had the chance to know people—whether friends or potential romantic partners —without the fear of them finding out about the videos and seeing me as just a sex object...just expecting I was good for nothing but fucking." He stared toward the window. "In the videos, I was always the bottom. Always the virgin. Always made to appear fragile and being taken by force. I know it was because that was what sold best—it was the persona they pigeon-holed me into—but just once, I'd like to experience sex that's soft, slow, gentle. Not that I don't want to explore hard, fast, and kinky with the right person, but I want the chance to decide who and when. I've never even gotten a blowjob because the studios always felt their audiences expected to see me sucking guys off and not the other way around—and Max sure as hell wasn't going to blow me." Shaw shook his head and tucked his chin to his knees. "At the time, neither studio I was with had started exploring the whole *twink tops* angle, so I definitely never got the chance to top. I'm not even sure it would be my thing, but that's just it, *I* want the chance to decide."

He sighed.

"I've had sex with so many people, but not a single one has truly been my choice. It's never been just us without the studio—the people, the camera, the lights—or my history being right there with us. I just want to be with someone who wants me for me. I left that film persona behind, I'm just Shaw now and I want the chance to be known and wanted as just Shaw."

A shaky laugh escaped him and he buried his face in his hands.

"And I have no idea why I told you all of that. Sorry, that was major overshare."

Finally, unable to ignore the urge any longer, I reached out and wrapped a hand around his calf. "You can tell me anything and everything, nothing is too big or too small."

"Thanks," he whispered.

"I need you to know I completely understand what you're saying about being in control of who you sleep with—hell, just being in control of *any* decisions...you spent a lot of years having no control over anything in your life, so I completely get what you're saying and why you need that control—but I want you to know I'm here." I brushed my thumb over his warm skin, the soft hair on his leg tickling under my touch. "Whether you need me here as a friend, or you want me here as something more, I'm ready and willing. And if I ever do or say anything that makes it seem like I'm taking away your control, let me know. I don't ever want to do that. Hell, even just putting the furniture in your room makes me wonder if that was overstepping."

"No," Shaw shook his head, "that was so nice. I'd probably still be sleeping on the floor if you hadn't helped with that. None of you guys have ever made me feel like I don't have a choice. Just the fact you include me in things, and I know I can always say no if I want to, is a huge thing for me."

"Good. We want you here. *I* want you here, want you to feel welcome and part of what we've got together."

We were quiet for a moment before Shaw spoke again.

"Is being my friend all you'd want?" he asked, his voice a mix of precious hopefulness and worry.

"Not in the least," I answered honestly. "I've wanted something more with you since the moment I laid eyes on you, but I'm not one to push someone into something they don't want. So, whatever happens next is all on you. But I'd kick myself in the ass if I didn't at least let you know I definitely wouldn't mind being a part of you getting to make decisions about who you sleep with."

Shaw reached down and took my hand, electric heat traveling through my body.

"If we were to let something happen between us, would you be willing to be with *just* me during that time? I've never had complete trust and monogamy, it's something I'd like to experience."

"I don't think I have it in me to share you if I ever get my hands on you," I said, my words gruff with emotion and desire. "And I'm not the type to be with more than one man at a time."

"Do you think you could put up with me kinda checking off the things I haven't done? I don't want it to seem like you'd just be a convenience for me to work through a checklist."

"I've had plenty of time to figure out what I like and don't like, I'm not in any rush for any reason. You need to work through a checklist? I'm a thousand percent on board with assisting." My balls ached with how badly I wanted to be the man Shaw chose to help him knock out some of his to-do list.

A thought struck me and I must not have done a very good job of hiding it.

"What?" Shaw asked, a worried look upon his face as he chewed his bottom lip.

"I guess, I just...in the interest of transparency...I understand this might just be you exploring, and I can be okay with that, but I need you to know I'm willing to commit to more than just exploring."

Shaw cocked his head. "Are you saying you don't want to be a trial and error test subject?" He grinned when I chuckled. "Not into *only* being part of a research and development project?"

"I'm saying, I'm down for whatever you need." I pulled his leg toward me, draping it over my side and pressing a kiss to his inner knee. "Friends-with-benefits while you fuck yourself in me and on me every which way 'til Sunday? I'm in. Dating while doing the same? Again, I'm in. You want a ring on your finger to feel safe and committed? Let me find the closest jeweler."

That gorgeous angel-on-earth face registered my words

and his eyes grew wide. "Did you just say you'd buy me a ring—like *marry me*?"

I smiled and pressed another kiss to the soft skin of his inner knee. "If that's what it takes. And I didn't say that to overwhelm you, I just need you to know I'm on board completely." Scowling, I nuzzled my nose against his leg, enjoying the scent of orange cream. "I get you may want to spend the next however many months and years eating at various buffets, but I'm at a point in life where I'm satisfied with the varied menu at my favorite sit-down restaurant."

Shaw opened his mouth, closed it, opened it again, and dissolved into giggles. "Did you just...oh god, I can't with you." Then he sobered for a moment. "Is it weird I really don't have any desire to explore things with other men? That's weird, right?" He gripped my shirt and pulled me up, his knuckles firm against my chest.

I ended up sitting on the bed between his spread legs, our mouths only centimeters apart.

"What did you do to me?" Shaw whispered. "It's like I took one look at you and my heart honed in on its target—locked and loaded. Shouldn't I *want* to be out experimenting with other guys? Sampling the multitude of buffets so to speak?"

Pressing my forehead against his, loving his legs wrapped around me, I sighed. "I guess I should do the respectable thing and tell you to sample all the buffets—and I *am* saying that, if it's what you want—but I'm not going to try to convince you to hit every single buffet in town if what you really want is on the menu at the sit-down restaurant."

Shaw's deep brown eyes locked on mine.

And then we both burst out laughing.

"Okay, okay, the buffet and restaurant metaphor needs to go. It's cringey as hell," Shaw said, his cheeks pink as he continued to giggle.

And then the smiles melted into a smoldering heat between us and Shaw's lips found mine. He shifted to straddle my lap, our mouths mating in a slick, promising dance. Shaw rocked his hips, rubbing our hardened lengths together, and we both moaned at the delicious friction.

I knew he needed to control what happened next, but damn if I didn't have some ideas of what I'd like to do to him.

"I want—" His words cut off with a gasp as he rocked into me again and my hands took hold of his ass.

"What do you want? Tell me," I demanded.

"Want your mouth on me, wanna feel your fingers in me." His words were desperate and sent fire straight to my cock.

Reaching for the hem of his shirt, I paused. "Is this okay?"

He nodded vigorously. "Yes, take it off. Take it all off."

In a frenzy of limbs and clothing, we found ourselves naked, and I pressed Shaw gently to his back. "Tell me again what you want. This is all you, I need to know every single thing you want me to do."

Shaw fisted his rigid length, a drop of pre-cum glistening on the tip. "I want you to suck me off and finger me. Wanna come in your mouth with your fingers in my ass. And then I want to watch you jack off on me."

Fuck.

I knew this kid was going to be the death of me, I just hadn't counted on how soon he'd be sending me to my grave.

"Just to make future discussions easier, I've been tested twice since my last sexual partner. Everything was negative." I moved to the edge of the bed and rummaged through the bedside table for a bottle of lube.

"Same. We got tested regularly at the studios. There was a case of chlamydia that spread through the guys once when I was at Benny's, but antibiotics cleared everything up. I was asymptomatic, but it showed up in the tests. Benny doubled up on tests for a while after everyone got the all-clear. Everything since has always been negative."

"Your call on any and all protection," I offered.

"It's all good," Shaw said, stroking his cock.

I tossed the lube onto the bed and settled beside him. "Let me take over?" I asked, my words a whisper against his soft lips as I moved his hand away and wrapped my fingers around his shaft.

I'd hear that whimpery groan every night in my dreams.

Shaw's hand snaked around my neck and pulled me in for a slow, sloppy kiss as I stroked him, thumbing over his leaking slit. No kiss had ever been so hot, so right. Tongues licked and mated, slicked over teeth, and battled for dominance.

When I cupped Shaw's balls, he broke the kiss with a hiss and thrust his hips, wildly seeking friction.

"Wanna taste you," I murmured at his ear. "You good with that?"

Shaw made a strangled noise and rolled his hips, fisting his hands into the comforter.

"Let me hear it," I said. "You okay with my mouth on your cock?"

"Yes," he hissed, his voice cracking as I pressed kisses along his jawline and down to his collarbone.

I stopped for a moment to play with his nipples, tongue and nipping, loving the way Shaw's body responded to my touch. Snaking my tongue over the ink on his chest, I made my way to his navel, dipping in to tease before swiping my tongue over the pearly liquid dripping from his cock.

When I took him in my mouth, I wasn't sure which of us groaned louder.

Sucking cock was something I enjoyed.

I guess it would be overgeneralizing to say all gay men

like to suck cock, but I was definitely one of the gay men who loved it.

But swallowing around Shaw's length had me wanting to bow down and worship him, offer up prayers of thanks in the name of gay men everywhere.

He was so damned perfect.

When his hand gripped the back of my head, pulling gently on my hair, I nearly nutted against his leg right then and there.

"Fuck, Julian," Shaw cried out. "Oh, fuck. Oh my god, that's so good."

I popped off his dick and reached for the lube. "You want my fingers?"

"God, yes. But just a warning, I'm not gonna last long," Shaw said, one arm thrown over his eyes as he looked to be trying to gather himself somewhat.

I stuffed a pillow under his ass. "Spread your legs for me." Slicking my fingers and his gorgeous hole, I threw the bottle aside and teased his tight pucker. Wishing for a moment it was my tongue, but knowing Shaw had to make that request, I inched into him, loving the way his body opened for me.

Maneuvering to take his cock back between my lips, I slid my finger deep just as his cock head hit the back of my throat.

Nearly gagging when Shaw's hips rocketed off the bed, I smiled around his shaft as he mumbled apologies and nonsense words about how good I made him feel.

"Give me more," Shaw begged, his hand fisting in my hair again as he fucked his dick into my greedy mouth.

With my balls aching for release and my cock smearing pre-cum all over Shaw's leg, I added a second finger, loving the way Shaw cursed and moaned. When I could go no deeper, I curled my fingers in search of that sensitive bundle of nerves.

Shaw's hips thrust up hard and fast as he cried out. "Fuck, Julian. Fuck. I'm gonna come."

I finger-fucked him, his ass tight and hot on my slick digits, and swirled my tongue around his cock before swallowing him.

He groaned my name as his body tensed, his hot release scalding my tongue, his ass clenching tightly around my fingers as his shaft pulsed between my lips.

Teasing over his prostate one last time as he unloaded in my throat, I gently slid my fingers from his ass and let his spent cock slip from my lips. "You good?" I asked against his lips when I moved up his body to kiss him.

Shaw wrapped his arms around my neck and devoured my mouth, tasting himself on my tongue and whimpering as he came down from his orgasm. "That was the best ever," he murmured against my lips.

I didn't remind him he had nothing to compare it to because I was feeling pretty damn proud of making him come so hard. "I'm available for *that* any time you need it."

"I wanna watch you jerk off on me," Shaw said, reminding me of his earlier request as he shoved the pillow from under his ass aside and pushed up on his elbows like he was getting ready for his favorite show.

"Where do you want me?" I asked, moving to my knees, my cock begging for release.

"Straddle my thighs," Shaw directed and I moved into the requested position. "Fuck, you're gorgeous."

I smiled, stroking myself and I gazed down at pure and utter perfection. "Right back atcha," I said. "This won't take long."

"Would you fuck me over a dresser if I asked?" Shaw said, his eyes darting from my cock to my face and back again.

"I'd fuck you anywhere you asked me to," I answered, gritting my teeth as my orgasm built.

"Would you let me fuck you?" Shaw asked, his words almost challenging like he thought I might balk.

"Fuck, Shaw," I hissed, pre-cum dripping onto his spent cock. "If you were hard right now, I'd sit on that pretty dick and take every drop you could give me."

"Shit, Julian." Shaw's words were breathy and raw. "Fuck, I want that. I want so much."

"I'll give you anything you want."

"Come here and let me suck you, wanna taste you before you come all over me." Shaw reached for me and urged me to move up his body.

When I reached his chest, he licked my leaking slit, his dark brown eyes never leaving mine as he opened for me and swirled his tongue around my cock head.

"Oh, fuck," I gritted out. "Fuck, Shaw." If he wanted me to come *on* him rather than in his mouth, he needed to stop what he was doing with his tongue.

He sucked on me for a moment longer before popping off and licking his pretty pink lips. "Definitely wanna continue that sometime, but move back down and come on my cock."

Never taking my hand from my dick, I positioned myself back on his thighs and stroked my shaft as I watched his face. When Shaw swiped a finger through the liquid leaking from my slit and licked it like it was the best thing he'd ever tasted, I couldn't hold out any longer.

The tingle teasing the base of my spine hit high gear as my balls drew up tight and my release exploded from me in long, creamy ropes onto Shaw's chest, his stomach, and his valiantly-trying-to-rejuvenate cock.

With a groan, I fell forward, catching myself on one hand while coaxing the remainder of my orgasm from my dick with long, slow strokes as it pulsed in my fist.

I dropped to my elbow, bringing my face as close to Shaw's as possible without kissing him. When he reached for my cum-covered hand and brought it to his mouth, I grunted as heated desire kicked me in the gut.

He licked my release from my fingers before capturing my mouth and plunging his tongue deep inside, sharing my flavor with me as his nails ran up and down my back.

Sated from orgasms, our kisses soon moved from hot and sexy to slow and sweet.

"We need to clean up," Shaw whispered. "I should go to bed."

"My bed is always open, but where you sleep is up to you."

"How about we play it by ear?" Shaw rolled from the bed and traced his fingers through the mess I'd made on his torso. "You wanna suck me off again in the shower?"

"I think I've created a monster," I teased as I stood from the bed.

A brief look of worry crossed Shaw's face like maybe he thought I didn't want to drop to my knees and suck his dick.

I wrapped an arm around him and pulled him close, kissing him deep and slow. "A monster I will *always* want to please. Don't you *ever* think I don't want your cock in my mouth."

Our shower took quite a bit longer than absolutely necessary, but we were both clean and well-sucked by the time we finally fell into bed.

The fact Shaw automatically followed me to my room and let me curl my arms around him as we settled under the blankets brought a smile to my face and had me wondering just what kept me going before this man walked into my life.

The next morning, faint noises from the rest of the crew moving around the apartment woke me up.

For a brief moment, I struggled to figure out why my arms and legs were all tangled. But a quick shift of my hips brought my morning erection flush with a very fine ass and I immediately recalled the night before with Shaw.

"You gonna keep teasing me with that or put it to use?" Shaw mumbled, pressing his hips into me, making my cock and balls ache.

"You have time?" I asked before taking his earlobe between my lips and sucking gently.

"We'll have to save long and slow for another time, but I'm definitely all for a quick fuck before work."

"I'll give you what you want, but don't ever think you're just a quick fuck to me," I said, my words gruff with both sleep and emotion. Maybe it was too much, too soon, but I needed Shaw to know where I stood. He was so much more to me.

Shaw turned his head over his shoulder and tilted his chin for a kiss.

The connection quickly morphed from soft and sweet to hot and deep.

"I want your cock buried in my ass," Shaw said, biting my lip. "And I wanna come on your fist while you fill me with your load. We may have to hurry before work, but you're a lot more than a quick fuck to me, too. I've been there, done that, and I have no interest in it."

Dipping my tongue into his mouth, I savored his slick heat before searching blindly for the lube. "Tell me what you want."

"I don't need a lot of prep, kinda love the idea of feeling you all day at work." Shaw reached for his ass and spread himself open for me. "Just go slow until I'm used to it. And I want you to jack me while you fuck me."

Well, all right then. Best damn wake up of my life.

I slicked my cock and his waiting hole, tossing the bottle aside. Pressing the head of my cock against his pucker, recalling how tight he was around my fingers, I groaned as I worked my length into him inch-by-inch.

"Oh fuck, Julian," Shaw whimpered, rocking his ass back and taking me deeper. He reached for my hand and moved it to his dick. "Jack me."

"Yes, sir," I teased, nipping at his ear. "You're kinda bossy."

"Sorry," Shaw said, not really sounding terribly sorry.

"Don't ever apologize for asking for what you want. It's hot as hell. I like you telling me what to do." I closed my fingers around his rock-hard shaft and stroked, loving the way he shivered in my arms and thrust his cock into my fist.

He draped his leg over mine, meeting my thrusts and grunting with each slide of my dick into his tight heat. We fell into the most perfect rhythm. My left arm tucked under his body, wrapped around his chest, and my right arm slung over his hips, stroking his throbbing cock.

Pressing a kiss against his neck, I fucked into him, knowing the prickling heat and pressure in my balls meant I wasn't going to last much longer.

"Fuck, Shaw, I'm gonna come. You want my load in your pretty little ass?" I asked, thrusting harder and faster, pinching his nipple and loving the whimpers escaping him.

"Please, Julian, please. Give it to me," Shaw begged.

I added a slight twist to my stroking fist, making him cry out and his body tense.

Shaw's release spilled over my fist, his ass clenching hard around my cock.

My orgasm tore through me, exploding hot and thick in his tight hole.

Breathing heavily, both of us lost in the high of what we'd just shared, we rode out the last pulses and jerks of our bodies as the sweat cooled on our heated skin.

"I realize that might not be an *every* morning type thing,"

Shaw started, pausing to catch his breath, "but I'm all for making it something we do from time-to-time."

"I'm down," I mumbled against his shoulder.

"Don't forget the top two things on my list right now…"

"I just shot all my brain cells in that load, remind me," I said.

Shaw chuckled. "You fuck me over a dresser—I want to take that back. And I get to play twinky top and fuck you." He turned to catch my eye. "If you're okay with that. I know I've got all these things I want to do, but I need you comfortable with them too."

"So. Fucking. Okay," I said, kissing him between each word. "Just tell me when and where. I'm one hundred percent vers and the idea of having that gorgeous cock in my ass is one I can get on board with for sure."

I glanced at the clock on the nightstand.

Shit, we needed to get a move on.

"Before our day gets away from us, I want to get a drink fest planned soon." I slid my hand up and down his arm.

"That sounds fun. Hopefully I'm not an annoying drunk."

"I'll be your designated driver—even though we won't be leaving the apartment. You can be as annoying as you want and I'll make sure you're safe."

"Thank you," Shaw whispered, shifting just enough my softening cock slid from his hole. "You guys are the only ones I'd trust."

"One more thing and then we totally have to bust ass," I said.

"Pretty sure you already busted my ass," Shaw teased and I couldn't help but smile at my soft, gentle angel.

"Can we plan a date? I want to do it right. I'll pick you up, take you to dinner and a movie, the whole thing."

Shaw squealed and wrapped his arms around my neck. "You are the most amazing man. I swear, Julian. There is so much goodness in you—and not just because you're making all of my little wants and wishes come true—you are truly just the kindest and most caring person I've ever met."

"Being kind and caring is easy—especially for you, you make me want to be the best version of me." I kissed his forehead, his nose, his lips. The kiss grew more intense and I wanted nothing more than to hold him in my arms the rest of the day, but real life wouldn't wait.

"Oh, Julian!" Leighton called from outside my door. "I'm worried about Shaw! He's not in his room. Wherever do you think he might be? What could have happened to him?" The door to my room cracked open just as I pulled the sheet up over our bodies.

Leighton's and Ollie's smiling faces appeared in the crack of the door.

"Oh, look, Ollie, we found our dear Shaw. He wasn't lost. He was just...well, I'm not exactly sure what's happening here. What do you think, Ollie?" Leighton was hamming it up for sure.

"Well, Leighton," Ollie chimed in. "It appears our precious Shaw found himself a lovely daddy bear to take care of him for the night. And by take care of him, I mean rail his ass into next Tuesday."

Shaw busted out laughing and buried his face in my chest.

"Get out, both of you. We need to get ready for work." I threw a pillow toward the door and huffed out a laugh when Leighton and Ollie yelped and ran off.

"Well, I hope you weren't planning on keeping things secret," I deadpanned.

Shaw shook his head. "No, I knew there was no chance of that." His big brown eyes met mine. "Is it weird I kinda want to tell the whole world we're together?"

"Are we?" I asked, hot emotion punching me in the gut. "Together?"

Shaw nodded solemnly. "I meant what I said, I need this to be just us. Dating? Boyfriends? Whatever you want to call it—if you're okay with it?"

"Dating, boyfriends, together, just us—we can call it anything you want, and yes, I'm completely okay with it." I kissed him again. "But you're going to be late if you don't hurry up."

"Worth it," he said, returning the kiss.

I ended up walking Shaw to work, backtracking to get him a hot chocolate from a smirking Leighton at Cravin'-a-Cup, and delivered it to him about fifteen minutes into his shift with a smile and a kiss before starting my day.

Clogged toilets, a busted pipe, and a resident bitching about being able to smell pot when the wind blew just right filled my shift, but nothing could have wiped the smile from my face or the contented feeling from my heart.

———

A WEEK LATER, Shaw quietly closed the door to my room and bit his lip as he walked toward me in just a towel. I'd just gotten out of the shower and we had just over an hour before Lucas was bar tending on the roof and the crew had promised to provide Shaw with his first night of drunkenness.

I grinned at Shaw as he prowled toward me. "Hi," I whispered against his lips when he wrapped his arms around my neck and pressed a kiss to my mouth. "How was your day?" We'd fallen into such an easy, enjoyable routine—our entire crew fit together so well, and Shaw had proven to be the missing piece in my otherwise contented life.

I hadn't been looking for love.

Hadn't felt the least bit unsatisfied.

But then Shaw had waltzed into my life and made me realize what had been missing.

The way my heart tugged in my chest every time he smiled.

The swirling in my gut whenever he was nearby.

The lava-like heat in my veins when I took him in my arms.

And, maybe more than anything, the extreme happiness making me feel as if I floated on air when we spent any time together.

Sure, we hadn't known each other long, but my heart recognized the difference between any relationship I'd ever had in the past and what was between Shaw and me.

I didn't want to push him into committing to forever if he wasn't ready for it, but if I had my way, we'd never know a future without each other.

Shaw ignored my question for a moment as he moaned into me and opened for my seeking tongue. When we finally broke the kiss, both breathing heavily, our towels not hiding the evidence of our arousal, he pressed his forehead to mine and smiled.

"My day was good. Got all caught up with my filing, had to call the police on suspected domestic abuse, kept a toddler company while his mom got stitches, and had lunch with Dean."

"I think I'm jealous," I growled.

"Of all the filing I got to do?" Shaw teased.

"Of Dean getting to eat lunch with you."

"Dean isn't getting to pretend I'm a virgin and fuck me over a dresser," Shaw answered, fiery heat flaming to life in his brown eyes.

I cocked a brow. "And I am?"

He nodded, his bottom lip between his teeth. "I want to take back what they took from me. It's my call, my choice, and I want to be the virgin you bend over the dresser."

Lashes fluttering, he studied my face. "If you're willing? And I don't want to play like it's against my will."

"Never done a lot of role playing, but I definitely have no problem taking this sweet ass on a dresser, and I'd never do anything against your will." I caressed hands down to cup his ass cheeks and squeeze. "Can I rim you first?"

Shaw rocked his hips against mine and whimpered. "Please."

"Grab the lube and move to the dresser," I ordered. "Lose the towel."

Shaw rummaged in my drawer for a bottle of lube before dropping his towel and moving over to my dresser. "Figured your room was the better choice since your dresser is shorter than mine. I'd need a chair to bend over mine."

Chuckling, I tossed my towel aside and moved to stand behind him. Catching his eyes in the mirror, I wrapped my arms around him and leaned my chin on his shoulder. "You sure you want to do this? Want me to be your first time?"

I felt Shaw's sharp intake of breath when he realized we were already playing, his heart thumping hard and fast in his chest.

"I'm afraid it might hurt, but I want it to be you," Shaw answered, his words shaky, whether in play or from real nerves.

"I'll make it so good," I whispered, running my hand down his torso and fisting his cock. "Your tight little hole will look so pretty stretched around my cock."

Shaw clung to my arms, his legs barely holding him up.

Gripping his chin, I pulled his mouth around to mine and devoured him, taking everything he had to give.

Stepping back slightly, I left him gasping for breath and pushed at his shoulder. "Bend over, rest on your elbows, and spread your legs. Gonna eat this ass and make it mine."

Shaw shivered and bent at the waist, resting his upper body on elbows and widening his stance.

Dropping to my knees, my hungry cock bobbing between my legs, I spread Shaw's ass and brushed a teasing finger over his hole. Loving the way he whimpered and thrust his greedy ass back, I pressed my face between his ass cheeks and swiped my tongue over his soft, pink pucker.

Moving my mouth lower, I sucked first one ball then the other into my mouth, swirling my tongue around the sensitive skin. Trailing my tongue from his balls back to his hole, I grinned as Shaw's knees buckled and bumped into the dresser.

"Whose pretty ass is this?" I asked before gathering spit on my tongue and spearing his tight hole.

"Fuck, Julian. Fuck, it's yours," Shaw whimpered.

"This virgin ass is gonna look so damn good stretched around me." I fucked him open with my tongue. "You ready to take this cock?"

Shaw rocked his ass against my face. "Yes," he gritted out. "Fuck me, please."

After one last swipe of my tongue against his sloppy, wet hole, I stood and reached for the lube. "You think your virgin ass can take this cock?"

"Yes," Shaw answered, his eyes meeting mine in the mirror. "I wanna feel your cock in my ass. Want you to be the first man to fuck me."

My heart twinged, hating that Shaw needed to play this game, but I was willing to help in any way I could. I didn't like to think of Shaw with other men and I was glad to pretend I was the first man to slide into his tight heat.

Slicking my shaft with lube, smearing the pre-cum around my head, and pressing a lubed finger into his well-rimmed hole, I smacked my cock against his pucker. "You ready for this? Gonna open for me and take my load?"

Shaw groaned and spread his legs wider. "Please, Julian."

I pushed into him slowly, loving the way his body opened for me. "Fuck, Shaw, you look so good on my cock." There was absolutely no playing around in my words. Watching the way he stretched open for me, knowing we were connected in the most intimate way possible, I lost myself to the beautiful picture before me.

He gasped when my balls pressed against him, my cock buried deep inside. "Oh god, Julian, it's so good." He took a few steadying breaths and then met my eyes in the mirror. "Lift my leg up and go hard."

My gut churned. I absolutely loathed the idea of sweet, innocent eighteen-year-old Shaw being fucked for the first time like that. But I understood he needed to make the scene his own, make the choice *his* and not some asshole director who saw him as only a money-maker. A gratefulness burned in my chest to know I was the one he'd chosen—the one he trusted—to take back this part of his life.

I lifted his right leg, letting his bent knee rest on the waist-high dresser top. Gripping his hips, I drew my cock out of his body and slammed back into him.

Shaw cried out and hissed, "Yessss. Just like that. Hard and fast."

"You want this? You want this cock? Want my load dripping from your ass?" I picked up speed and rocked my hips into him as the dresser wobbled under the movement.

"Yes, yes, yes," Shaw answered in rhythm with my thrusts.

"I'm gonna fill you with my cum and then suck you off while you fuck my face," I promised, knowing my orgasm wasn't far from the surface.

"Please, Julian, wanna feel your cum in me."

Sweat trickled down my back as I watched Shaw's face in the mirror. Pure ecstasy lit his features and I wanted to carry him to the bed and make love to him soft and slow just as much as I wanted to pound into him over and over. "Fuck, Shaw, I'm close."

"Give it to me," he begged.

Snapping my hips, loving the tight heat of his body around my cock, I let the orgasm wash over me as I shot my load. With my dick still pulsing out every last drop, I bent to rest my chin on his shoulder and took a moment to catch my breath. "Can I suck you off?"

Shaw's eyes sparkled with desire as he nodded.

"Come over to the bed," I directed as I gently pulled from his body.

I moved to my bed and settled in the middle with my head on a pillow.

"Straddle me and fuck my face."

Shaw's eyes registered what I was asking him to do and he stroked his leaking cock before climbing over me and settling his ass on my upper chest. "Never got to do this," he said, his words almost reverent as he smeared his pre-cum over my lips. "Open up."

My lips parted and my greedy tongue lapped at his slit before he shifted and pressed his shaft deep, the head of his cock bumping the back of my throat as I swallowed around him.

Shaw pulled out. "Is that okay?"

"Yeah, it's good. Fuck my mouth and shoot down my throat."

Shaw groaned as he shifted on his knees and grabbed the headboard before slipping his cock back between my lips.

The kid needed no instruction on how to face-fuck and he was grunting out his release all too soon. I took every drop he gave me, savoring his flavor as his balls slapped against my chin.

"Holy fuck," Shaw said as he collapsed next to me, throwing an arm over my waist. "That was fucking amazing."

"Mmhm," I grunted.

We enjoyed the quiet for a moment.

"Thank you," Shaw whispered. "That's the memory I want seared in my head and you made it happen."

"Anything you need. All you have to do is ask. I'll be here, ready, waiting, and willing."

"Ready to get me drunk?" Shaw asked, lifting his head so I could see his glorious grin and gorgeous brown eyes.

"Let's get your drink on," I said, smacking a hand against his ass and laughing when he squealed.

We walked out onto the rooftop to a sea of smirks and knowing grins.

I didn't even care because I knew damn well Jett and Leighton either fucked each other's brains out before the party or would be getting down and dirty after the party—or both.

And even though I wanted nothing to do with knowing about my brother's sex life, I was pretty sure Ollie and Bash had taken things to the next level—or would be very soon.

"Alright, alright, alright," Lucas called from his little makeshift bar in the corner of the rooftop. "Shaw, my man, come on over and let's get this party started."

Everyone put in their orders for the drinks they wanted—I stuck to water—and Lucas got everyone set up. Then he set to work providing Shaw with a variety of samples.

We'd bought build-your-own packs of beers and ciders, two red wines and two white—dry and sweet of both—and Lucas had provided much of the liquor for shots and mixed drinks.

"Are you sure you don't want to drink?" Shaw asked me. "You could probably have a beer or a shot at least."

"I'm good. This is your night."

He wrinkled his nose. "I just feel bad you're not getting to drink."

"I don't *need* to drink to have fun and I'm more concerned about making sure you're okay. This is your night, your chance to let loose and try something for the first time. I'm here to make sure you're safe."

Shaw leaned into me, tucking his face against my neck. "Thank you," he mumbled as I brushed a kiss over his brown hair before he took a seat on one of the stools.

Lucas led Shaw through the beers—which he hated—and the ciders—most of which he liked. Leighton and Ollie sat at the bar flanking Shaw and trying everything as well.

Dean hovered and helped Lucas.

Jett and Bash sipped their drinks and watched their men.

And I stood protectively behind Shaw as he sampled everything Lucas put in front of him.

The plan was to let him taste a little of everything and then let him have full-size drinks of some of what he liked without mixing liquor, beer, and wine all together.

Since Shaw hated the beers, liked the ciders, hated dry wine, and liked sweet wine, we moved easily into the hard liquor.

"Okay, I'm going to give you half shots just so you know what they taste like," Lucas said, pouring tiny shots of rum, whiskey, tequila, and vodka. "After this, you can either have more of the ciders or sweet wines, *or* I can fix you some mixed drinks I think you'll like."

"But not all of them," I interrupted. "You'll likely have a hangover anyway, but mixing all the different drinks together is just asking for trouble."

Lucas gave me a wink and ruffled Shaw's hair. "Your daddy guard dog is right, once you decide what you want to drink, you need to stick with it. That's why I made all these samples so small." His pointed look my way was a clear *Duh, man, I know what I'm doing*. "Didn't want you sick." Lucas leaned in and pretended to whisper, "And I didn't want Papa Bear here on my ass."

Shaw leaned back against my chest and tipped his face up for a kiss. "Papa Bear can be on my ass anytime," he murmured against my lips which made me smile at the fact he was already getting tipsy and made Leighton and Ollie bust out laughing.

"Can I call you Papa Bear?" Leighton asked.

"Not if you expect me to answer," I said back, patting his cheek.

"Jettie-boo," Leighton crowed. "Can I call you Papa Bear?"

"No," Jett answered, scowling, but a smile played on his lips as he tipped his bottle up for a drink.

Shaw shivered and yucked his way through the shots and declared he wanted Lucas to make him all the pretty drinks. His tolerance for alcohol would maybe increase if he found himself partaking a lot, but he was definitely on the lightweight side of things for the time being, and I was glad we were all with him to make sure he was safe.

While Leighton, Shaw, and Ollie laughed about something, I cleared my throat and caught both Lucas's and Dean's eyes. "Easy on the pours, maybe, yeah?"

Lucas winked. "I gotchu, babe."

Two hours later, Shaw had exclaimed each pretty drink Lucas handed him to be his favorite of the whole night and he'd giggled his way through each one as the crew visited, joked, and just enjoyed being together.

It truly amazed me how perfectly the eight of us fit into each other's lives—almost like something brought us all together on Cravenwood Block, like destiny or something.

"Julian," Shaw whispered—quite loudly and everyone bit back chuckles—as he hung on my arm sipping what he'd been sad to discover was just water once we'd determined he needed cut off.

"Hmmm," I answered, keeping my arm around him because we'd discovered quickly that buzzed Shaw—and then *drunk* Shaw—tended to get too close to the edge of the roof for our comfort.

And he didn't seem to have any worry about falling in the pool.

Or the hot tub.

He was also very quick for an inebriated person.

So, keeping him close to my side was my plan for the rest of the night.

"My lips are tingly," he said, smacking his lips together and making a popping noise. "Ohhhhh, there's something wrong with my teeth. They're numb. Is it bad if I can't feel my teeth?" He made a biting motion, gnashing his teeth together, his big brown eyes meeting mine with worry.

"Pretty normal, but it's a sign you definitely need to be done drinking for the night."

"I always advise cutting off alcohol *before* you get to the numb teeth phase," Lucas said as he cleaned up the bar and packed his supplies into totes he and Dean would carry downstairs a bit later.

"Good idea," Shaw said, nodding solemnly. "I'll put that in my notes. Stop *before* your teeth are numb. *Definitely* stop when you notice your teeth are numb. Even though it may be too late." He pretended to write in a notebook and we all snorted in laughter. "Ohhhhh, everyone get out their phones."

"Why?" Dean asked.

"I watched this show that was on in the waiting room the other day. This family had a person go missing—he'd gotten sick, like a medical emergency or something, and wasn't answering his phone—but they'd all shared locations with each other so they were able to track him and get him the help he needed." He waved his phone around. "We need to do that. Just in case. You never know when one of us might be in trouble."

I almost thought one or two of the guys might balk, but everyone just shrugged in agreement and pulled up the group text. Once we'd all shared our locations and been notified the others were doing the same, Shaw seemed content and we pocketed our phones.

Shaw stood in my embrace popping his lips and clacking his teeth, lost in his own little world, swaying to music only he could hear.

"You have fun tonight, baby doll?" Leighton asked, patting Shaw's cheek.

"So much fun," Shaw answered with a hiccup and a giggle. "You guys are the best, you know that. I love you all so much."

I maneuvered him to a lounge chair and pulled him down to stretch out beside me. Shaw instantly curled into my side.

"Especially you," he whispered—again, loudly enough for the whole crew to hear. "Love you. Shaw and Julian, Julian and Shaw. I do, you know? Love you." He patted my chest and rested his head on my shoulder. "Ohhhhh, closing my eyes is a bad, bad thing. I'm all spin-y. Why are the rest of you not spin-y with numb teeth and tingly lips?"

"We didn't drink as much as you and we've all had more time to build up a bit of tolerance," Bash offered as the whole group gave me a range of looks over Shaw's profession of love. "Although, I don't think Ollie and Leighton are too far from spin-y."

Ollie and Leighton were definitely giggly and glassy-eyed. I had no doubt they'd be dealing with hangovers in the morning as well.

"You think he'll remember that in the morning?" Lucas asked, tipping his chin toward a now snoring Shaw.

"Nah," I answered softly. Not that his claim of loving me hadn't gone straight to my heart and dick, but I knew he was drunk, so I wasn't putting much stock in his words. "People say a lot of things when they're drunk."

"But if he meant it? Remembers it and says it when he's sober?" Lucas pushed.

"Let him be," Dean interrupted. "Maybe it's private."

Lucas gave Dean a look. "What? We're all friends. I want them to be happy. There's nothing wrong with that."

Dean threw an arm around Lucas's shoulders and pulled him into position for a noogie. "I'm just saying, maybe Julian doesn't want to share all about their relationship."

"Sure didn't seem to mind when we could all hear that headboard bangin'," Leighton said with a giggle.

"Like you're one to talk," I shot back with a smirk.

"True, true," Leighton conceded. "I know I'm not the quietest."

Jett snorted and pressed a kiss to Leighton's head.

We chatted for a bit longer, but soon it was time for me to get my sleepy little drunkard into bed. As the rest of the crew gathered our belongings and tidied the rooftop, I shifted to stand and jostled Shaw.

"Shaw? You ready to head to bed? We need to get some more water and Tylenol in you so the hangover isn't as bad."

Shaw just mumbled something and snuggled into the lounge chair.

"Come on," I said, hefting him to a sitting position and pulling him to stand.

He was pretty much out of it as I led him down the stairs and into the apartment.

"You need to pee?" I asked him, figuring I'd just get him to bed and he could shower in the morning.

"Oh god," Shaw moaned. "Julian?"

"Yeah?"

"My teeth aren't numb, but now I feel like I'm going to puke."

"Toilet to your left. I'm right here," I said, helping him to his knees just as his stomach decided to rid itself of the entirety of his first night of drinking.

There was little I could do aside from make sure he stayed upright as he heaved and get a washcloth ready for his face.

Several minutes later, when he seemed to have nothing left to bring up, I helped him stand and wiped his forehead, neck, and mouth.

"Gotta rinse my mouth," he mumbled, reaching for the faucet and swishing water from his cupped hand around in his mouth.

"You think you're done? Wanna sit here while I get you water and Tylenol?"

Shaw shook his head. "No, think I'm good. I'll get in bed —gotta piss first."

I left him to take care of things and grabbed water and medication from the kitchen. By the time I returned, he was in his room, stripped down to just his boxers, climbing into bed.

"Will you stay in here with me tonight?" he asked before taking the water and pills from me.

"Yeah, but no sex. I don't want to do anything when you're not completely with it." I shucked my clothes, leaving my underwear on, and climbed into bed with him.

"Pretty sure my dick is out of commission anyway," Shaw said with a chuckle.

"I'll have to get up earlier than you. You can sleep as long as you need since you and Dean have the late shift tomorrow." I pulled him close as he cuddled into my side.

"Mmhm," Shaw answered. "Thanks for tonight. It was

fun and I'm glad we did it. Not sure I want to get *this* drunk again and I'm pretty sure tomorrow will confirm that, but it was good trying everything and getting to experience it all with my safety net."

"No problem. Glad we were able to make it work."

"I meant it, you know?"

"Hmmm?"

"I do love you," Shaw said, propping himself up on an elbow. "This is probably the worst time to be declaring my love because you think I'm drunk and I just puked up a gallon of alcohol. But I do love you." He swallowed hard and traced a finger from my brow to my temple and across my lips. "At first, I worried I was just infatuated because you were gorgeous and kind and treated me so well, but it's more than that. You mean something to me. *This* means something to me," he said, gesturing between us. "If it's too soon for you, I understand, but I need you to know how I feel."

Pulling him to my chest, I pressed a kiss to the top of his head. "I love you," I whispered, gruffly. "This means something to me, too."

Shaw was asleep long before me.

I spent at least an hour smiling into the darkness and thanking whatever god would listen for sending me an angel.

SEVEN

Shaw

___

"SHAW, SOMEONE'S HERE FOR YOU!" Leighton called from the front room. "And he's *hot*. Got that nice guy, sizzling daddy vibe going on." He laughed as Jett grabbed him around the waist and pulled him onto his lap on the couch.

I walked out of my room—after spending much too long deciding on black skinny jeans, a fitted black and white t-shirt, and a black denim jacket along with lace-up black boots for my first-real-date-attire—and nearly swallowed my tongue to see Julian at the door looking all dapper with a bouquet of flowers in hand. He was wearing dark wash jeans, a black button-up, and his nicest black work boots.

"Hi," I whispered, letting him pull me close for a kiss and not caring at all the rest of the guys were watching. Sure, the whole *first real date* thing happening *after* we'd fallen into bed and declared our love was maybe a bit backward, but it still meant the world to me that Julian was putting so much into making my dreams come true and helping me block out the past with new memories of the present.

"Awww, they're so damn cute," Ollie cooed. "This is the shit romance is built on." He sighed and let Bash tuck him under his arm. It had actually been adorable as hell to watch their relationship as it evolved.

"Julian," Leighton said, pretending to be serious. "I think I speak for all of us when I ask what are your intentions with our Shaw?"

Julian bopped Leighton on the head with my flowers. "I intend to take him out to eat and to watch a movie. Then I intend to bring him home and spend the entire weekend in bed. If that's okay with you?" My stomach fluttered at the thought. Would the floaty, in-love feeling ever go away? I wanted to bottle it up and bathe in it.

Leighton rubbed his chin as if thinking it over. "Yes, that meets my approval. But we do have to ask you treat him like the angel he is."

"Wouldn't have it any other way," Julian said.

Leighton hopped up and took the flowers from Julian. "I'll put these in water for you."

"Make sure you use my vases," I said, biting my lip to hold back a silly grin. I had vases for flowers now and it made me ridiculously happy. Thanks to a man who did something so kind for me even back when I was nothing more than a roommate.

Knowing Leighton would take good care of the enormous bouquet, I let Julian lead me out the front door and through the door to the the stairway.

Letting out a little squeak of surprise when he pinned me to the wall and cupped my face in his hands, I quickly melted into the kiss. Julian's body pressed against me. His hot, seeking tongue explored my mouth as if promising what was yet to come and his hands held the sides of my head, thumbs caressing my temples and cheek bones.

"If we didn't already have reservations and movie tickets," Julian said, his words gruff when the kiss finally ended, "I'd take you back to our room and finish that."

I touched my fingers to my lips. "I think I'd let you."

He smiled and nuzzled his nose against mine. "I love you." His words over my lips.

"I love you," I repeated, still in awe of how much my life had changed since the moment I stepped onto Cravenwood Block.

Julian took my hand and we made our way down the stairs, out of the building, and to a car waiting to take us into Midtown for dinner.

The meal ended up being a lot fancier than either Julian or I would probably ever opt for again, but as first real dates with the man you love go, it was highly enjoyable. The best part of the night—aside from the private corner, flowers, sweet red wine—which I now knew I liked—and holding Julian's hand—was sharing crème brûlée and laughing with him over something stupid.

The movie was just as amazing. We sat in the back row, held hands, and laughed until we cried at the ridiculous comedy. Despite not being super hungry, we split a popcorn and Coke because Julian said it was all part of the real date experience.

As we walked back home, opting to enjoy the night instead of calling for a ride, Julian gave my hand a squeeze. "So, another item off your list. Did it live up to expectations?"

I smiled and bumped my hip against his. "Honestly? It was so much more. But I think that's because it was with you. I could have done the whole date with some asshole and it would have been the worst night of my life. But spending the evening with you, knowing you worked so hard to make it special, it was absolutely perfect."

"Best date I've ever been on," Julian said. "But you're right, the company was what made it work so well."

We walked quietly for a moment before he spoke again.

"I'm sure you've got other things on your list, and I'm not doing things *just* to check them off…" He trailed off.

"What?"

"We've got all weekend and I meant what I said about keeping you in bed—obviously, only if you're on the same page." He opened the door to Cravenwood Apartments and walked us to the elevator, saying hi to the few people in the lobby area.

When the doors slid closed behind us, I wrapped my arms around his neck and let my lips hover over his. "Are you suggesting maybe I get the chance to play twinky top?"

Julian grunted and pressed his hips against mine. "I'm saying I'd be down for anything and everything you might have in mind."

The elevator doors slid open and we made our way to our unit.

"Any chance you think everyone is in bed and we can just casually walk to our room without interference?" I asked.

Julian laughed out loud. "Not a chance in hell."

We spent the next thirty minutes telling the others about dinner and the movie before Dean brought up the text we'd all gotten a while back.

"Hey, you get any more of those texts?" he asked.

I bit my lip and felt Julian's shocked expression as it locked on my face.

"Shaw?" he asked, concern lacing his words.

"Only a couple. Maybe three or four. They've just been stupid stuff like *You messed everything up* and *Does your boss know what you used to do?* I've saved them, but nothing has been super threatening, so I blocked the number and just ignored them."

Julian's arm went around my shoulders and he pulled me close. "You should've told me. I know you can take care of yourself, but we can help. You don't have to hide stuff and you don't have to face shit like that alone. We're here." He pressed his lips to my temple. *"I'm* here. Text me, call me, scream for me. I'm here."

"Oh my god," Leighton exclaimed. "That's your song. When we have our prom, you can dance to it."

"What song?" Jett asked the question we were all thinking.

Leighton jumped up and spread his arms wide. "'One Call Away' by Charlie Puth. We'll do a Night Under the Stars theme. Since it's Shaw's prom, their song will be the feature. It's an amazing song and it fits perfectly."

Grateful for the change in subject, I glanced at Julian.

His smile and shrug told me he'd do whatever he needed to make me happy and his earlier concern was just because he loved and worried about me.

"Perfect." Leighton clapped his hands together. "Would y'all be okay with me wearing a dress?" He propped his hands on his hips. "I saw this amazing dress the other day and immediately thought about how I should have worn something like it to my own proms." He sat down on Jett's lap. "Would it bother you?"

Jett's arm protectively wrapped around Leighton's waist. "You know I don't give a damn about what you wear. You do you like always and I'll enjoy the ride."

"Oh, I'll give you a ride," Leighton teased and Jett's eyes flamed.

"Ohhhh, I'll do this look I saw with a tux jacket and a skirt," Ollie piped up. "I love the idea of us all getting to be more ourselves at this prom."

Bash took Ollie's hand and my heart soared because me asking for a prom at twenty-four was possibly giving everyone else some sort of an opportunity they maybe missed out on back then.

We chatted a bit about decorations, food, music, and attire before Julian and I declared our exhaustion.

Leighton snorted. "Yeah, right. *Exhausted*. Not yet, but probably will be soon—at least after a couple rounds. Maybe we should have a competition to see who can be the loudest."

"Please, god, no," Dean groaned.

Leighton and Ollie cackled.

"Maybe everyone just needs to fuck each other's brains out and you won't notice how loud others are being," Ollie suggested, waggling his brows at Dean.

A *very* interesting look crossed Dean's face just as Lucas cleared his throat and stood up. "I'm going up to the roof to work out. See you fuckers tomorrow."

The group dispersed with a round of good nights.

Julian and I opted for separate showers so we each had a bit of private time.

"Just so you have an idea of what I'd like tonight to look like," I whispered against Julian's lips as we traded places in the bathroom. "I'd like to top and then switch if it works out. If not, we can flip for round two. We can play it by ear, but I really want to know what it's like to be inside you." I smacked a kiss to his mouth. "*And* I'm greedy. I'm not going to pass up the chance to have you in me."

"Fuck," Julian grunted, reached for hips and pressed our cocks together. "Yes."

"To which part of it?" I asked, smiling against his lips.

"Any of it. All of it. Just fuck, yes." He kissed me long and slow. "I wanna see you stroking your cock on my bed when I get out of the shower. I won't be long."

"Take your time. I'll be waiting."

By the time Julian came into the room, locked the door, and left his towel hanging over a chair...dear god, the man was gorgeous...like seriously. He wasn't solid muscle or hung like a horse. He was truly heading into *dad bod* territory, but it worked for him, and very much worked for me. He had an average sized dick—but the main thing was he totally knew how to use it—and his build wasn't going to win any ridiculous modeling competitions, but he was *mine* and I loved every inch of him. From the way he protected me, to the way he understood my need to make my life my own again, to the smile he saved for just me—this man was a treasure and I sometimes worried I was dreaming.

But his strong, warm arms wrapped around me and I knew he was real.

"I thought you were supposed to be on the bed stroking yourself," he grumbled in my ear.

"I was, but I got too close," I said, feeling sheepish I'd almost blown my load before the show even got started. "So, I decided to light some candles and get the lube out. Needed a moment to cool down."

"Little edging never hurt anyone," Julian teased. "Came pretty close in the shower, just thinking about what you wanted to do."

"On the bed, ass up," I said, smacking his rear and laughing when he grunted in shock.

"Just gonna shove it in? Thought you'd take a bit more time, have a little finesse," he teased as he crawled onto his bed on his hands and knees, dropped to his elbows, and spread his legs.

I moved behind him and pressed his hips down before stretching out on my stomach and spreading his ass cheeks. "Not sure rimming is part of finesse," I said before swiping my tongue over his pucker, "but I plan to enjoy it." Moving to his taint, I lapped at the sensitive skin as he wriggled and moaned. "This okay?"

"Fuck, Shaw," Julian groaned. "Yeah, it's good."

I returned to licking, swirling, and teasing his hole,

gaining more confidence with each moan my mouth elicited from my conquest.

When Julian started thrusting against the bed, I pressed a final kiss to his entrance and rolled him to his back. "Nope, no coming yet. I have plans for this," I said, licking over his leaking cock head. My own dick screamed for release, my balls drawn up tight as I reached for the lube.

Realizing my hands were shaking, I dropped the bottle, sat back on my knees, and took a deep breath.

Julian pulled me to him, bringing us chest to chest. "You okay?"

I huffed. "Yeah, just nervous I guess. Maybe there's a reason they never let me do this."

"Hey," he cooed, cupping my face in his large hand. "Forget them, forget all of it. This is you and me. I want you, any way I can get you. If this is what you want to do, I'm down—like, *really* down—but if you decide against it, that's fine too. There're no requirements here. Hell, we can rub off on each other just like this and fall asleep with our jizz sticking us together for all I care." He pressed a kiss to my lips. "I love *you*. Nothing changes that."

I took a shuddery breath and buried my face in his neck. "That was beautiful and I love you too, but there's only one problem."

"What's that?" Julian asked, a smile in his words.

"Well, your sweet words went straight to my dick and I want to be inside you more than ever now."

Julian laughed. "And this is a problem?" He handed me the lube. "Chop, chop. My ass is yours."

I'd never been so emotional and turned-on at one time in my life. Slicking my cock nearly sent me over the edge and I was grateful for the few moments it took to smear lube on Julian's hole while I worked him open with slippery fingers.

"You okay with this position?" Julian asked as he spread his legs wider.

"If you are. I really want to watch. See your face when I'm in you." I bit my lip and pressed my cock head against his hole.

Julian threw his head back with a moan. "God, yes."

His tight heat gripped me as I worked myself into his ass. "Fuck, fuck, fuck," I muttered, hissing against the waves of pleasure washing over me as I watched Julian's body open.

When my balls pressed against him, I paused and dropped to his chest, tears stinging my eyes.

"Hey, hey," Julian soothed. "I've got you. You're doing so good. Feels so good."

"It's fucking amazing," I murmured against his lips. "Thank you. I'm just being sappy and I'm going to blow within a minute the second I start moving."

Julian chuckled. "No worries. I'll switch you places if you're up to it. Fucking you while your load drips from my hole definitely sounds good."

His words made my dick twitch.

Wrapped in his arms, buried in his heat, I'd never felt as protected, loved, and on fire as I did at that moment. It was sensation overload and I never wanted to lose the perfection of what we had together.

I'd had no clue what to expect from my first time topping, but the rush of emotions—wanting to mark him as mine, wanting to savor every moment, never wanting to let him go —were overwhelming.

While I already had plans for a time when we'd go hard and fast, the gentle thrusting of my hips sliding my cock in and out of Julian's tight hole was absolutely perfect for the time being.

And definitely enough to have me within seconds of blowing my load.

The thought of Julian's body stretched around me as I pulsed my release was all it took. With a final thrust of my hips, my orgasm washed over me and jets of cum pulsed from my cock, filling him with every last drop.

Julian's legs tightened around my waist, his hands cupping my ass and holding me tight against him as my balls emptied. "Fuck, Shaw," he groaned, his ass clenching around my shaft. "Beautiful," he whispered. "When you're ready, I need you to jack me, blow me, or get on your back so I can be inside you. Unless you want to ride me."

I chuckled against his neck and my cock gave one more twitch. "Riding you would be amazing if I had any energy left, but I think I'm gonna have to just spread my legs and let you fuck me."

"Do you trust me?" Julian asked as my soft cock slipped from his body.

"Mmhm," I mumbled, rolling to my back.

Julian rolled from the bed, slicked his cock and my hole, and positioned my ass at the edge of the mattress. "You need fingers first?"

"Nope, I prepped in the shower and there are no muscles left in my body now," I answered lazily, totally ready for Julian to slide into me while I just laid there and watched, enjoying all the fruits of his labor.

He pressed his cock head against my hole and worked his way in as I whimpered, my exhausted body greedily accepting him.

Julian leaned down and hooked his arms under my shoulders, lifting me and turning around to press my back against the wall. I cried out as the cold surface hit my back and Julian's cock pressed the rest of the way in.

"Fuck," I moaned, my arms tight around Julian's neck. "Fuck," I repeated, clearly reduced to only one word as he fucked me deep.

As he pinned me against the wall, Julian's hands cupped the sides of my head, our eyes meeting in a fiery gaze. "I love you, Shaw," he whispered, the weight and truth of his words settling in my soul.

"Love you." My words slurred with emotion as his steady thrusting continued, my dick somehow coming back to life as if I hadn't just blown my entire being five minutes earlier.

Julian's rhythm picked up speed and intensity—I chuckled briefly as I wondered if the entire apartment could hear me being fucked against the wall—before he paused and moved me back to the bed.

Placing me in the middle, Julian's body pressed against me, his hips moving in a wicked grinding motion as the scent of our sex filled the air. "Fuck, Shaw," he growled in my ear. "I can feel your cum leaking from my ass."

I groaned at the picture his words painted, loving the idea of my seed dripping from him. "I'm gonna come again."

Julian grunted and fucked me harder. One final rotation of his hips had me crying out as a gentle orgasm took me. Julian's body tensed, his cock throbbing in my ass as he filled me with his hot, pulsing release.

We lay together for what seemed like hours, breathing heavily, hands caressing, lips pressing tiny kisses. When Julian eventually pulled from my body, we both shivered and groaned.

He made his way to the bathroom and returned with a wet cloth to clean us both up a bit. "Was gonna suggest a shower, but I don't think I have it in me."

"Sleep now. Shower later," I murmured as I moved under the blankets. "Maybe you can fuck me awake in the morning —use the leftover cum as lube."

"Fuck," Julian growled as he joined me under the covers and pulled me tight against him as his little spoon. "Keep talking like that and I'll be ready to take your sweet ass again in five minutes."

"Five minutes, huh?" I teased, knowing there was no way either of us was getting it up for at least an hour.

"Okay, maybe not. But come morning? Your ass is mine."

"Ass, body, heart…everything about me is yours," I murmured.

"And everything about me is yours," Julian said, his words tickling over my ear.

We fell into a blissful sleep.

And come morning, Julian made good on the promise to own my ass again.

———

A FEW DAYS LATER, I was on my lunch break, catching up on emails and social media while I ate a sandwich and chips Julian had sweetly packed for me the night before after I got so wrapped up in a book I'd forgotten.

My phone buzzed with a text.

Unknown Number: Blocking me won't work. You need to understand what you've done. You need to lose everything like I lost everything.

Me: What do you want? This is getting ridiculous.

SERIOUSLY, while I hadn't thought blocking Luka's first number would end it, I was irritated he'd started his shit again so quickly.

. . .

Unknown Number: *I want you to admit you ruined my life. I want restitution. I want you to lose everything. I want the world to know you're a dirty little whore.*

Me: *Give it up. I'm not coming back to you. I've moved on from the films. I owe you nothing.*

Unknown Number: *Stupid little bitch. I will always find you. Come to your precious library and talk to me like a real man instead of the cowering, gutless crybaby you are.*

MY GUT CHURNED.

Clearly, ignoring and blocking wasn't working.

Luka was a mean-ass piece of shit and he'd decided how he wanted this to play out whether I liked it or not.

But if I met him in an open, public place, I didn't think he'd hurt me. He liked his money, sex, and reputation—albeit shady and dubious—too much to do something right out in the open and face jail time, or even any extra attention from the law since he already barely avoided a permanent spot on their radar.

Maybe I needed to just have it out with him. Let him rant and rave while I stayed calm. When he was done dressing me down and trying to threaten me into coming back to his low-rate studio, I'd tell him no and let him know I was going to the police with his texts. Filing a police report and requesting a protective order maybe wouldn't fix the whole situation, but I could at least take a step in the right direction.

Taking a deep breath, I thumbed out a response.

. . .

Me: I'll be there in ten minutes. I'm willing to listen to what you have to say, but I'm not changing my stance. I'm not coming back to the industry. It's not what I want or need at this point in my life.

Unknown Number: *Would have been nice if someone had asked me what I wanted or needed.*

PART of me wondered what was up with Luka holding a grudge for so long.

I knew I'd made him money, but I wasn't the only guy he could get for his films. Granted, a lot of adult film actors were looking toward the higher-end studios with top-notch reputations and Luka's was *not* that, but he still would have had no trouble finding guys to replace me.

Hell, I *knew* he'd replaced me within a couple days of me dragging my broken body out of town. The four brand-new videos he'd posted within a couple weeks proved the point.

So, why was he still so hung up on making me pay?

Feeling silly, but knowing Julian would be upset if I didn't tell him what was going on, I texted him.

Me: The texts started up again. Luka wants "restitution" for ruining his life. I'm meeting him in the library yard in ten minutes. Just wanted you to know.

JULIAN WAS likely busy at work, but he'd see the text when he took a break.

I'd grown a lot in the last several years and I knew I could handle the situation myself—even if my stomach acted like it was attempting to turn itself inside out—but letting Julian know what was going on just felt right.

Not because he demanded it or wanted to control my every move, but because I knew he loved me and wanted to know I was safe.

I still had about thirty minutes of my forty-five-minute lunch break, so I threw away my trash and pocketed my phone before crossing the street and heading toward the library.

The walk was short and as I made my way toward the library, something caught my attention in my peripheral. Turning, I couldn't help the grateful hiccup of relief that bubbled from me when I saw a very determined Julian making a beeline for me.

When he was close enough, he reached out and yanked me flush against him.

"You came," I mumbled into his chest.

He grunted and leaned back to catch my eye. "Of course, I came. I will *always* come for you. No matter what." He kissed me soundly before brushing a chunk of hair from my face. "You sure you want to do this?"

Even as he asked, he took my hand and began walking toward the library yard. He knew it was something I needed to do and he was going to stand with me.

My protector, my support, my forever.

"I think I need to show him I'm done. I'm not going back. I'm not backing down. I'm living my life and I've moved on, he needs to do the same thing. Maybe he just needs to see me and hear me say it's over before he'll give up on this infatuation." I squeezed Julian's hand. "Thank you for being here. I *can* do this myself, but having you here makes it easier."

He squeezed back. "Always."

We made our way into the little courtyard area.

There were several people walking to and from the library. Some were eating lunch under trees. Children played on the playground.

I didn't see Luka.

Hairs on the back of my neck prickled with anticipation of how this was going to go.

Maybe it was a mistake.

Had Luka lost his grip on reality?

Would he try to harm Julian or me?

"Couldn't even show up without your bodyguard?" The voice dripped in nasty anger, but I didn't recognize it.

Turning toward where the words had come from, I saw a woman standing near the circular stone wall of the courtyard.

Realization washed over me.

It wasn't Luka.

Hadn't been Luka this whole time.

Rebecca.

Pastor Elijah Stone's wife.

The foster mother who stood by while her husband knocked me around and left me battered and bruised more often than not.

"You?" I couldn't help the confused disgust in my voice.

"Me," she answered with a wicked sneer.

"How did you find me? Why did you even *want* to?" I crossed my arms over my chest, taking comfort in knowing Julian was right there, and fighting the shock and anger swirling through me. I hadn't seen the woman in *years*, but she clearly had some hang-ups regarding my effect on her life.

"I kept tabs on you after your filthy lies got my husband taken away. I know the sinful smut you've been up to. You're going to burn in hell and I'll laugh as you scream." Rebecca's wide eyes burned, her skin coated in a sheen of sweat.

"*You* stood by and let your husband beat the shit out of

me. If I'm burning in hell for some movies, I guess I won't be burning alone."

"He's not my husband anymore," Rebecca shrieked, drawing curious attention from some onlookers. "Thanks to you and your lies, I watched my husband be carted off to jail. My kids lost their father. I lost my place in the church." She patted her hair as if attempting to regain her composure. "I've found a new church, of course, but my Elijah left me when he got out of jail; he's moved on with some slut he met in *therapy*—the homewrecker is pregnant with his child now. My children won't speak to either of us. All. Because. Of. You."

"Yes, *me*," I scoffed. "A *child*. A child who had lost his mother and his first foster family. A child who needed love and protection and instead got beaten and verbally abused on a nearly daily basis." I felt Julian shift beside me, antsy and tense. "But sure, your fucked-up life is *my* fault."

"Elijah just wanted to raise you right—" Rebecca started.

"Don't *even*. He beat me and shamed me with Bible stories. No child deserves what he did—no child deserves a sorry excuse for a mother who stands by and lets it happen. I always wondered why—was it because he beat on you and the kids before I showed up? Better the runt little foster kid than you and your own?"

Rebecca's wild eyes focused for a moment, but she barreled on. "I'll get you fired. I'll ruin your life the same way you ruined mine."

"How are you going to rat me out without admitting to the fact you've been watching gay porn?" I cocked my head to the side and studied her. She had aged quite a bit since I'd last seen her. Her heavy breathing and wide eyes added to her completely unhinged appearance. "I've never once been ashamed of the work I did. Whether it was to survive or because I enjoyed it, I'll tell anyone about my past in the industry. Hell, we can walk over to my job right now and tell my boss. Guarantee she won't give a damn because I single-handedly saved her ass when I took over at the front desk. But yeah, let's go have a chat. After that, we can go to the police station. You probably better have a list of all the porn sites you've found me on ready to disclose—or maybe they'll just confiscate your phone and computer."

I paused to let the thought sink in.

"Are you still in the little house with the blue shutters?" I asked.

Rebecca frowned. "Yes, why?" she sneered.

"I just need to know where to send the police when I make a report against you and request a protective order." I tapped my chin. "Are you working now? Since your dear pastor left your pathetic ass, did you have to, *gasp*, get a job? No more Suzy Homemaker, huh? She's a working girl now." I cocked my head and watched the fury storm over her features. "You'd think you'd understand the need for me to do whatever was necessary to survive." I shrugged. "But since you want to play the tattletale game, how about I return the favor by letting your job and your new church know *all* about your past and your current obsession with stalking me—oh, and don't forget the porn. So. Much. Porn."

Rebecca gave a little growl. "Stop saying that. It's not as if I enjoyed that filth. I only watched it to track you down and gather blackmail. No one would believe you. I'm a *Christian*, you're nothing but a dirty slut." She gestured toward me and a wedding ring glinted in the sun.

I couldn't help the snort of laughter. "Ohhhhh, Elijah left you, but it looks like you had no trouble moving on, huh?" I motioned toward her left hand. "Does new hubby know he married a stalker who likes to watch gay porn? What would he think of the fact you let Elijah beat me so badly I lost a permanent tooth and had to wear casts for broken bones?"

I shook my head and stepped closer, smirking at the way she took a step away.

"No, we're not doing this. You're going to open your phone, let me delete my number and my friends' numbers and the texts. Then you're never going to contact me again because if you do, the report I'm making today and the no contact request I'll ask for, will all come into play if you ever bother me or my friends again. You don't even live anywhere near here so you're going to leave and never step foot on Cravenwood Block again. If you do, all of your secret past will be shared with anyone and everyone who will listen—pretty sure you've got a whole lot more to hide than I do, don'tcha think?" I moved closer again and held out my hand.

For a moment I thought Rebecca was going to lunge at me or verbally attack, but as quickly as the flames of anger flared to life, she deflated—all the energy leaving her. Defeat replaced the rage as she handed over her phone opened to the texts.

I deleted the texts and the numbers before holding it out to her. "You got a second chance when he left you. I'm sorry your kids left too—they had to do what was best for them—but you need to take a look at what you want your future to be and move towards making that happen rather than living in the past. I meant nothing to you then and I'm nothing to you now. Focus on what's actually important—plotting a revenge that won't even affect me isn't the best use of your time and energy."

She dashed at tears which seemed to be a mixture of frustration and returning anger before yanking her phone from my hand. She walked away mumbling something about dirty sluts and payback—there was a very good chance she wasn't done, but making the police report and asking for a no contact would hopefully help.

Julian put his arm around me as we watched her get in

her car. He casually held up his phone and took a picture of her license plate. "You did so good," he said, his words gruff with emotion as he pressed a kiss to my head.

I sighed. "It felt good. The pastor got punished, but she never did. It was good to tell her all that and see she's been hurting too. But I don't want to focus on revenge and punishing the people who hurt me. I just want to make new memories and enjoy the journey we're on. We've got too much to look forward to to let someone like her mess it up." I knew I may have only bought myself time before Rebecca tried some shit again, but it wasn't something I wanted to think about right then.

"Prom is coming up," Julian said with a smile. "I think LuLu invited us to dinner soon. And I maybe have a surprise for you."

"A surprise? What is it?" I asked, cuddling under Julian's arm. I had to get back to work. I knew filing my report with the police would be a stressor within the next day or so, but for the time being, I was with the man I loved while we made plans for our future.

"Wouldn't be a surprise if I told you." Julian chuckled and kissed the top of my head.

"Will I like it?"

"I think so."

I smiled and did my best not to wriggle with happiness as we headed back toward the health center. Between prom, dinner with LuLu, and a surprise, I wasn't sure which I was more excited about.

Mostly, I was blessed to have Julian by my side.

When I'd walked onto Cravenwood Block, I'd had hopes of making a change in my life. I'd had no idea I'd find such security and happiness.

But I guess it's true what they say, love will always find a way.

Bonus Scene 1

"Shaw?" Julian called from the front door. "You ready?"

I took one last glance in the mirror, smoothed down my classic black tux jacket, and smiled. Would I have been this excited and nervous for my prom in high school? Probably worse. But I knew no prom back then would have meant anything close to what this one meant.

My date wasn't just my date.

Julian was my forever.

The men I lived with weren't just my roommates.

They were my friends, my brothers.

"He's the one, Mom," I whispered into the empty room, emotion shredding my words. "I'd give anything to have you back, but I'm finally safe and happy. He's the most amazing man, I know you two would love each other."

Swallowing thickly and blowing a little kiss to my mom, I straightened the folded square of deep purple cloth in my pocket and walked out to meet Julian.

Only Dean was still in the apartment—the rest of the guys were waiting for us up on the roof—but he'd been assigned to take pictures of Julian and I seeing each other for the first time.

I knew my friend and coworker was there, his phone pointed at us, but my eyes were only on Julian.

He looked…

Dapper.

Distinguished.

Devastating.

It was a simple black tux, his cummerbund, tie, and pocket square a purple just one shade lighter than mine, but he took my breath away.

Tears stung my eyes as I walked toward him, letting him take my face in his hands and brush a kiss over my lips.

"You okay?" he asked softly.

Nodding, I chuckled. "Just a bit overwhelmed and emotional. This night means so much to me—not just some dance, but the fact you guys went to all the trouble to give me something I'd missed out on." I reached up and traced a finger along the curve of his ear. "And you look amazing, kinda made me forget how to breathe."

Julian smiled and kissed me again. "I get that, you had the same effect on me. You're absolutely gorgeous."

Dean cleared his throat and excused himself to the roof. "See you up there."

We stood wrapped together for several moments, breathing each other in, enjoying the warm, comfortable silence between us.

"I believe we have a prom to attend," Julian said, offering me his arm and leading me out of the apartment to the stairway.

"Ready?" he asked as we reached the door to the rooftop.

The guys had been hard at work setting everything up.

The theme was A Night Under the Stars and Leighton was possibly going to flutter away in his excitement. I hadn't been allowed to see any of the decorations. I knew the theme and the main song—I also knew what Leighton and Ollie were wearing even if I hadn't seen them *in* their outfits—but other than that, I had no idea what to expect.

Julian nuzzled his nose against mine. "Let's go have ourselves a prom."

He swung open the door and let me step out onto the rooftop.

"Oh my god," I whispered.

The entire area glowed under twinkling lights and glittering stars while soft music played. Black and gold decorations sparkled in the lights as black tulle and gold silk rippled in the evening breeze.

It was absolutely breathtaking.

Picture perfect.

And these men had done it all for me.

Simply because I'd never had the experience.

Luckily the light coating of mascara Leighton had encouraged me to wear was waterproof because tears spilled from my eyes.

"Hey, Betty Boop," Leighton cooed, dabbing at my tears before pulling me into a hug. "Dry those tears, we've got a whole night ahead of us."

He laughed when I spun him away from me, his slinky black dress fluttering.

Jett caught him and dipped him low, a fiery look—definitely more than just sex—passing between them.

"Well, what do you think?" Leighton asked, clasping his hands in front of his chest as he stood back upright, body glitter sparkling under the tiny lights.

"It's beyond amazing," I choked out. "Thank you all so much for doing this for me."

"It started for you," Ollie said, "but I think it ended up being something all of us were looking forward to just as much as you." His fitted, short black tux jacket stopped just above a gauzy, poofy silver skirt that fell just above his knees. Strong, fit legs flowed into black, heeled boots.

Both men oozed confidence and happiness, and they looked amazing in their gender bending looks.

Not as amazing as *my* man, but close.

Jett, Bash, Lucas, and Dean all sported classic tuxes.

Jett's accessories matched the dark pink of Leighton's wrist corsage.

Bash's accent color was the same silver as Ollie's skirt.

While Lucas and Dean didn't look as if they'd *planned* to match, their burgundy and cream accents complimented each other perfectly.

"We clean up real good," I said, reaching for Julian's hand. "So, what does one *do* at a prom?"

"Well, from past experience," Lucas started, "it's a lot of standing around."

"Sneaking off to take shots," Ollie added.

"Smoking behind the school," Jett offered.

"Making out it the bathroom," Leighton said.

"Didn't any of you actually dance at your prom?" Dean asked. "I danced. It was fun."

Julian laughed. "I danced. Wouldn't say it was fun. Overrated is more the word I'd choose. If I remember correctly, it was hot, crowded, loud, and the music wasn't great."

"Well, welcome to A Night Under the Stars where your memories of prom will be happy forevermore." Leighton flourished his arm through the air. "We have a light dinner awaiting us—thank you Lucas for providing the eats. We'll take photos in front of the backdrop—I brought the tripod for a group photo. There's punch and cake. And we'll dance the night away."

Maybe some people would have thought the whole

scenario was childish and ridiculous, but it meant everything to me. Wiping away another tear threatening to escape, I took Julian's arm and let him lead me to the table for dinner.

The night actually turned out to be even better than I could have imagined.

Somehow, simple bar food and champagne was the most delicious I'd ever tasted. Same with the cake and punch.

We laughed so hard we cried during photographs and I knew without a doubt I'd be making a memory book for each of us.

The dancing was the best. Between acting ridiculous during the fast songs and savoring every moment wrapped in Julian's arms during the slow songs, I never wanted the night to end.

We'd listened to "One Call Away" by Charlie Puth once during dinner, but Leighton started it again toward the end of the night.

The words really were perfect for Julian and me.

As we softly sang the words to each other, swaying together under the stars, the most amazing calm settled over me. *This is absolutely perfect, this is my forever* washed over me in waves.

When the song ended, Leighton's playlist switched to a more upbeat remix of it and we ended up jumping around and laughing ourselves silly. That version flowed right into a different remix and Ollie ushered us all into a circle where we swayed and bellowed the words with our arms wrapped tightly around each other's shoulders as we crooned about how we'd always be just one call away.

Leighton paused the music. "So, I may have gone a bit overboard with the number of times I've played this song, but it's so good and it's *so* Julian and Shaw. I've got one more version and I expect everyone to dance and enjoy the last song of the night."

Lucas and Dean had joined in with the fast songs all night, but had only twirled each other around and joked while the rest of us slow danced.

However, as the first notes of Leighton's last "One Call Away" started, Lucas held out his hand to Dean and pulled his best friend close.

The rest of us watched, wrapped in our lover's arms, as Dean tensed and froze with his chest pressed against Lucas's.

Just when I thought Dean would back up, turn it into a joke, and spin Lucas around the dance floor, he wrapped an arm around his friend's waist and held his right hand up.

Something passed between them as Lucas mirrored the motions and they fell into a slow sway while a very sneaky Leighton had the song repeat without breaking the men from whatever little bubble they were in.

"They look good together," I whispered.

Julian nodded. "They do. I'm not sure what's best, but I'd love to see them both get their happiness—especially together."

I wanted that too.

I wanted the same perfect love I'd found with Julian to be something all my friends found.

Jett and Leighton had found it.

Bash and Ollie were well on their way, if not already there.

If it was meant to be, I so badly wanted Lucas and Dean to see what was right in front of them.

As the song came to an end, Lucas pulled Dean into a hug, pressing his face into Dean's shoulder. I wanted to say it was more than a platonic hug, but maybe it truly was just a hug between friends. Just because I wanted them together didn't mean it was what either of them wanted.

Sure, I'd seen some looks pass between them when the other wasn't looking.

Sure, they were attached at the hip.

And they had an entire lifetime together.

But that didn't mean they were a love match.

Of course, there was nothing pointing to them *not* being a love match either.

"You scheming over there?" Julian asked.

I bit my lip, trying to hide a smile at being caught. "Maybe. I know it's not our place and it has to happen on its own, but…"

"But we should leave our friends alone and let whatever is supposed to happen, happen," Julian said.

I sighed. "I know. You're right."

Didn't mean I wasn't going to be secretly cheering them on.

"What would you think about ending our prom night with a shower and bed?" Julian asked, nuzzling his nose against my ear.

"If that shower leads to a little *fun* in bed before we crash, I'm all for it."

Julian laughed. "Pretty sure that can be arranged."

Bonus Scene 2

"Oh god, Julian," I moaned as he worked me open with the new dildo he very much refused to hear was *just like Ollie's*.

My cock throbbed, smearing pre-cum on my stomach as Julian worked me open. I'd gotten him to go along with buying the silicone toy, complete with suction-cup base like the one Ollie had, by promising to fuck him with the dildo in my ass.

While he pressed the dildo in slowly, Julian took me in his mouth, swirling his tongue around my cock head and sucking as my balls drew up tight.

"Fuck," I gasped, fisting his hair. "You'll make me come if you keep that up. If you want me in your ass, you need to climb on."

Julian popped off my cock and slicked me with lube.

"Think that's going to stay put?" he asked as he straddled me and reached for my dick, moving it to press against his hole.

Between the dildo in my ass and Julian's tight heat engulfing my cock, I was barely coherent, but I nodded.

"Yeah, for now. Next time, maybe a plug or one of those cock rings with the prostate massager we saw. I'll get one like—"

Julian slapped a hand over my mouth and stopped grinding his hips on me. "If you say anything about he who shall not be mentioned during sex, I'll get off this train right now."

"Choo-choo," I teased.

He laughed and began the slow grind again, making me whimper. When he reached back and gripped the dildo, pushing back in the bit that had slipped out, I threw my head back and thrust up with a groan.

"Oh god, do that again," Julian begged, his dick leaking onto my stomach as he rode me and fucked me with the toy.

I thrust my hips up again and again, savoring each and every one of Julian's grunts and groans.

"You're going to come in my ass. Gonna clench that tight little hole around this dildo," Julian said. "Then I'm going to slip my cock between those pretty lips and come down your throat."

The promise of those words sent me over the edge and I cried out as my release barreled through me, my ass gripping the silicone as I unloaded into Julian's body.

When I'd finally stopped shuddering, Julian slowly worked the toy from my ass before pushing up on his knees to allow my spent cock to slip out.

He shifted up my body to straddle my chest, smacking his dripping cock against my lips. "Lick me."

Shivering at the command, I swiped my tongue over his slit before opening my mouth and taking him deep to the back of my throat. Julian gripped the headboard and shifted so he was up on his toes, thrusting his hips and fucking my mouth.

His tight balls smacked against my chin as his cock slid between my lips.

"Fuck, Shaw, so close," he growled, dropping to his knees to take his cock in hand and jerk himself until he painted my face. Sliding back in between my lips, Julian fucked my mouth until his orgasm subsided.

He rolled from bed and grabbed a cloth, wiping the majority of his release from my face before pulling me close for a long, slow kiss.

"Well, if lunch with LuLu gets me that each time, I'd like to request a standing invitation," Julian said, chuckling against my lips.

"Oh my god, what time is it? Are we going to be late?"

"Despite *feeling* like I just had hours and hours of sex, neither of us actually lasted very long and we still have time for showers before we need to leave," Julian said.

"Thank god, I definitely wasn't going to lunch with cum drying on my forehead," I said.

An hour later, we pulled up in front of the restaurant LuLu had picked for her birthday dinner.

"Come in, boys," LuLu exclaimed. "Oh, it's so good to see you. You're simply glowing." She leaned in close and whispered, "You'll have to let me in on what has you looking so vibrant."

Julian choked on air as his cheeks caught fire.

LuLu laughed. "Oh, I see. Well, I'll have to look into adding *that* into my regimen."

"What regimen?" Ollie asked as he walked over to greet us.

"Just my beauty routine. Shaw and Julian were telling me about what they use to keep their skin looking so gorgeous."

"Facials," Ollie deadpanned. "Gotta make sure you're getting those facials."

I truly worried Julian was going to expire on the spot.

"Boys," LuLu said, clapping her hands to get everyone's attention. "Thank you all for coming."

The entire gang was there. LuLu, Julian's and Ollie's dad, Jett's grandpa and his boyfriend, plus all eight of the Cravenwood crew.

A few moments later, all twelve of us were seated in a back room and asked our drink orders.

"Now, I picked the buffet because it's got a lot of variety and I figured everyone could find something they liked," LuLu said. "Feel free to grab a plate and dig in."

"I thought we'd escaped the buffet metaphor," I teased as we went to stand in line at the salad bar.

"I think buffets are fine for elderly birthday lunches," Julian whispered, "but I have no interest in them outside of actual meals."

"Menu at your favorite sit-down restaurant is good enough for you?" I said, laughter trying to escape.

"No place else I'd rather eat." Julian tipped my chin and caught my eyes. "For the rest of my life," he said pointedly.

"I have no need to go to another restaurant when I have everything I could ever want right here."

"Damn, you two really know how to beat a metaphor to death, huh?" Ollie asked with a smile.

I giggled and Julian pulled me to his side, kissing the top of my head.

"I'll gladly spend the rest of my life beating metaphors to death as long as you're by my side," I said.

"Even the one about facials keeping your skin looking great?" Leighton piped up. "I hear those protein *facials* are really great for the pores."

Julian groaned.

Several of the guys choked back laughter.

LuLu just caught my eye and winked.

Pretty sure she was onto us.

Bonus Scene 3

"Where are we going?" Shaw asked, excitedly wriggling in his seat while blindfolded.

I'd purposely driven him around Cravenwood a couple times in hopes of throwing him off our destination.

"You'll find out soon enough, nosy."

I'd had the idea for a while, but I had to wait until the manager let me know they had several of the items I thought Shaw would want. Once I'd gotten the call, I'd set the plan in motion.

Parking my work truck in front of the store, I hopped out and went to the passenger door. I helped Shaw out of the truck and grabbed his hands when he went to remove the blindfold.

"Hang on," I said, pressing a kiss to his nose.

"Aren't we here? I want to see where we are. I'm dying to know what the surprise is."

I laughed. "I know. You've been giddy for a week since I told you it was a go."

Sometimes, I watched Shaw in awe of what he'd overcome. How mature and courageous and determined he was despite all that had been taken from him, all that had been forced upon him.

But then I'd see him almost childlike as he experienced things he'd been cheated out of or recreated memories to replace the utter shit he'd gone through.

Today was one of those moments and I waffled between feeling good I could give him this surprise and being pissed he hadn't had someone to take care of him and give him surprises since his mom.

As my angel-on-earth bounced on the balls of his feet, looking sexy as sin in his tank and tight jeans, his tattoos only adding to the look, I placed my hands on his shoulders. "We're going to go in here and you're going to get to pick *one* item. It's kinda a specific category of items, but I'm not telling you until we're in there."

"Is this a sex shop?" he blurted.

I couldn't help the bark of laughter. "No, but if you want to be surprised with a sex shop, I can probably make that happen too."

"Sorry," he answered, ducking his head as his cheeks pinked. "But that would be kinda fun. Maybe we could take the guys."

Clearing my throat, I said, "Not sure I'm ready for eight of us in a sex shop. Not sure I'll ever want to shop for sex toys with my brother."

"Have you seen the dildo he—"

I clapped my hand over his mouth. "For the love of god, please stop. I do not want to hear about my brother's dildo."

Shaw laughed wickedly. "What if I got the same one? Would you overlook me referring to it as Ollie's dildo if I let you slide it in? Watch me fuck myself on it?" The little menace bit his lip and leaned in close to whisper. "Maybe I'll put it in and then fuck you while it stretches me open."

"Holy fuck. Okay, surprise is canceled. We're going home." I grabbed his elbow.

"No!" Shaw yelped as he laughed. "I'll be good. Promise. I want my surprise."

"Okay, but we're revisiting that. Like I said, you can pick one item. Only one and it has to be from a certain category. I'll take the blindfold off once we're inside."

I led him to the door and opened it.

Shaw's head cocked when the sounds of the shop hit his ears.

Knowing he'd figure it out any second, I slipped the material from his eyes.

He gasped. "Julian," he whispered. "Are you serious?"

"A cat. Just one. Preferably not a baby. The guys are already on-board." I gestured toward the area of the shop where about ten cats slept, played, ate, and watched us.

We walked toward the felines.

"Take your time. If you don't see one—"

"This one," Shaw declared as he saw a floofy black cat with two different colored eyes. "I want him."

"You didn't even look at all of them," I protested.

"I. Want. Him."

"How can you even know? You know nothing about him. You didn't even give the others a chance."

"Can I get two?" Shaw asked, lifting his chin in defiance.

"I think one is best to start with."

"Then I want him."

I pinched the bridge of my nose. "How can you know?"

Shaw stepped in close, our chests pressed together, his soft words tickling my ear. "I knew the moment I saw you that you were my person. I didn't know you. I wasn't looking for love. But my heart beat differently from the first second I met you. And I know this cat is my cat. I didn't need to know your history or anything about you. I felt it in my core we were meant to be together. That's what I feel for this cat."

I glanced toward the lady at the front counter who was clearly trying not to eavesdrop and doing a poor job of hiding her smile. She just shrugged. "That pretty kitty is completely ready to go home today. He won't do well with dogs or small children, but he'll be great with adults. He'd likely be fine with another cat, but he'll enjoy being the center of attention most of all."

"What's his story?" Shaw asked.

"Well, from what we could gather, he was orphaned and then taken in by a nice family. But something happened and they had to surrender him. His next home wasn't a very safe environment and that's how he ended up here. He's been here for a bit, just waiting for the right family." She smiled as she turned to get a folder of paperwork.

"Julian," Shaw croaked.

"I know, babe," I answered gruffly, pulling him close and pressing a kiss to the top of his head. "I know. I get it now."

Shaw nodded, clearly emotional as he swallowed down tears. "Can I hold him while we shop for his supplies?"

The lady looked surprised. "You can try. He might be a little skittish."

Within five minutes of Shaw getting the floofy black cat in his arms, the animal was curled into his chest, purring, eyes closed as if he didn't have a care in the world.

He'd found where he belonged.

On Cravenwood Block.

Just like Shaw.

———

On Cravenwood Block continues with Lucas & Dean- AVAILABLE HERE!

Also by A.D. Ellis

Jett & Leighton: On Cravenwood Block- a steamy, opposites-attract, bisexual-awakening, roommates-to-lovers M/M romance featuring a sexy-as-sin tattoo artist and a fresh, flashy barista with a smile that lights up the room.

Ollie & Bash: On Cravenwood Block- a steamy, opposites-attract, roommates-to-lovers, boss/employee, age-gap M/M romance featuring a man not looking for love and a younger music director with no filter.

Lucas & Dean: On Cravenwood Block- a steamy, friends-to-lovers, bisexual awakening M/M romance featuring lifelong best friends.

Holly Hills Christmas- Holly Hills Christmas is a steamy, feel-good, M/M age-gap holiday romance.

The Perfect Blend- A steamy, M/M age-gap, marriage of convenience, coffee shop romance

Perfect Timing is a steamy, M/M romance with an introverted, demisexual writer and a big, soft teddy bear of a nurse trying to navigate a love they've always dreamed of but most definitely weren't expecting.

Adore (Remington Place 1) is a steamy, age-gap, bi-awakening, dad's best friend M/M romance with a sassy smartass and a sexy silver fox. It's the first book in the Remington Place series and can be read as a stand-alone.

Crave (Remington Place 2) is a steamy, friends-to-lovers, fake relationship M/M romance with a virgin nursing student and a gruff, grumbly construction worker.

Desire (Remington Place 3) is a steamy, age-gap, hurt/comfort M/M romance featuring a heart-of-gold mechanic and a twink who's a lot stronger than he realizes. *Please note: This story has mention of sex trafficking and sexual abuse.*

Yearn (Remington Place 4)- a steamy, enemies-to-lovers, forced proximity M/M romance between two EMS workers who have hated each other for a decade.

Power Struggle is a steamy M/M, age-gap, forced proximity romance set in a small town. A twenty-year history, rival schools and jobs, and a hotel with only one bed make for a hot and heavy, sweet and sexy, HEA-guaranteed love story.

Take Me Home M/M age-gap, opposites-attract romance with plenty of steam and a scene that will make you appreciate camouflage and work boots

Let Love In M/M age-gap, forced proximity, dad's best friend, bisexual-awakening romance. Available on AUDIO!

Let Love Win M/M brother's best friend romance. Available on AUDIO!

Buried Secrets Romantic suspense stand-alone title. Available on AUDIO!

Silver in the City (3 books- meet the Silver crew you read about in Forged in the City) Available on AUDIO!

Forged in the City (3 books- a spin-off series from Silver in the City) Available on AUDIO

The BJ Boys Series (3 books, small town, big love) Available on AUDIO

Forever Better Together (friends to lovers) Available on AUDIO!

His Reluctant Cowboy (age gap, opposites attract, cowboy romance) Available on AUDIO!

What Blooms Beneath (LGBT Fantasy romance) Available on AUDIO!

Sawyer

(this was the first M/M I wrote and you may remember Sawyer and Luke being mentioned in Barrett & Ivan as well as in Ryker & Gavin)

The <u>Something About Him</u> series has been revamped with revised stories, updated blurbs, and spiffy new covers.

The series is available on ALL of your favorite book platforms!

Bryan & Jase

Brody & Nick

Barrett & Ivan

Braeton & Drew

Ryker & Gavin

Kade & Cameron

———

A.D.'s first stories (all male/female except <u>Sawyer</u> which is male/male) are in the Torey Hope and Torey Hope: The Later Years series. Find the 8 book box set HERE or you can find each individual title on Amazon.

For Nicky

Because of Beckett

Christmas in Torey Hope

Loving Josie

Decker

Sawyer

Zach

Kendrick

About the Author

A.D. Ellis is an Indiana girl, born and raised. She spends much of her time in central Indiana as an instructional coach/teacher in the inner city of Indianapolis, being a mom to two amazing teenagers, and wondering how she and her husband of over two decades haven't driven each other insane yet. A lot of her time is also devoted to phone call avoidance and her hatred of cooking.

She loves chocolate, wine, pizza, and naps along with reading and writing romance. These loves don't leave much time for housework, much to the chagrin of her husband. Who would pick cleaning the house over a nap or a good book? She uses any extra time to increase her fluency in sarcasm.

A.D. uses she/they pronouns.

Sign up at http://www.subscribepage.com/ADEllisNewsMMRomance for a FREE books!

Website http://adellisauthor.com/

Find me EVERYWHERE at https://www.adellisauthor.com/mylinks/

Connect with A.D. Ellis

Follow my website http://www.adellisauthor.com or find me on Facebook

http://www.facebook.com/adellisauthor

If you want to get updates about releases, interviews, sales, giveaways, and more please sign up for my newsletter http://www.subscribepage.com/ADEllisNewsMMRomance

Check out my TikTok- https://www.tiktok.com/@adellisauthor

You can also find me on Twitter http://www.twitter.com/ADEllisAuthor

Find me on Spotify if you'd like to listen to the playlist for this book (mainly just the songs I listened to while writing). Just search for A.D. Ellis.

To make it easy, find me EVERYWHERE here- https://www.adellisauthor.com/mylinks/

Acknowledgments

It's always so hard to write this part because I'm worried I'll forget someone without meaning to.

Readers- you are the reason I write. As long as you continue reading my stories, I'll continue writing them. Thank you for your support.

Bloggers- your support, reviews, and promotion are very much appreciated. Thank you!

My author buddies- I don't know that I could keep doing this without our brainstorm sessions, laughter, road trips, meals, wine, and friendship as my support.

Thank you to my alpha readers, betas, editors, proofreaders, and ARC readers! Your eyes and input are beyond important to me.

Brett and Gage- as usual, I doubt you even grasp how much your support, input, and friendship mean to me. This author journey has brought many wonderful things into my life, and you both are two of the BEST! I'm blessed to call you friends.

My family and friends- thank you for your love and support, always.